potent ash

potent ash

LEONARD KIBERA
and SAMUEL KAHIGA

EAST AFRICAN PUBLISHING HOUSE

PUBLISHED BY THE EAST AFRICAN PUBLISHING HOUSE
KOINANGE STREET, P.O. BOX 30571, NAIROBI, KENYA

PRINTED IN LETTERPRESS BY afropress ltd. P.O. BOX 30502,
SALDANHA LANE, NAIROBI, KENYA

CONTENTS

CONTENTS

For

Father and Mother

one

a silent song

Slowly the youth groped towards the door of the hut. He crawled weakly on his knees and elbows. The pain in his spine and stomach rapidly gathered violence. Suddenly, sharp pangs from his navel tore into his body and for one short, tormenting moment he was paralysed. Then the pain disappeared. It vanished with the same savage fury of its onslaught; left him cold with sweat; left no other mark really, as if it had never been there. But he knew it had only recoiled for another attack. Once more, he gave up the fight, let go his chin, and hit his forehead on the dirt of the flea-ridden floor.

He did not know what time it was but he was hungry. Not that time ever mattered. In the gloom of his eternal night, such things as time, day, or beauty, had no meaning. Flat and almost imperceptible, they were for him impossible and lay beyond the bitter limits of darkness. His world only responded to what he could feel and hear, and run away from. For it seemed to Mbane now as he slumped his youth in horror under the weight of closing death, that his short life had been one of retreat. Crawling away on his lameness, he tackled the world around him negatively and never hit back.

He thought about his new life away from the streets of the City. His brother, a preacher, had picked him up there, bringing him to this hut which felt so serene, yet so suspicious. It was not just the lack of the urban ruggedness and noise; or the lack of quick footsteps of busy people prancing away fitly to business he never understood, but who would occasionally answer his plea to keep him alive with a drop of copper in his hat. It was not just the feel of the air and wind whizzing through the trees around his new confinement. He could tell that there was meaning in his brother's silence of late, something strange, and yet perhaps well intentioned in his voice when he spoke. He could tell it too, when his brother repeatedly said, "I rescued you from that barbaric City so that you can see the light of God."

Somehow, however, he did recall the City with a kind of nostalgia. Not that he really knew it. In fact he had earned his living on one street only, retiring to the back lane when the street became deserted.

But the street had come to mean his life. It is true that he could not tell how long, how wide, how beautiful, how big it was. These were things which would not matter. He had become used to the talk of bright weather, lovely morning, or beautiful sunset, small talk which he could never share. Pedestrians would sing to the blue sky, whistle to the gay morning as their footsteps sang their way down the pavement, and this would taunt him. Still, he would be happy. For it was the gay people who mostly answered his plea. He had come to know how much money was the essence of urban life. Dull people, heavy tired footsteps and voices, betrayed anxiety, empty pockets. He had come to know, too, what day and night meant to them. When the sun poured its heat too generously upon him and the flies crawled along the edges of his lips, good men and women spent their time working inside the building next to him and many more up the street. It would be a dead night when the sun withdrew he knew not where, to yield the street to hostile cold. He would then steal into the back lane, unsheltered but undisturbed, to surrender his vulnerability to sleep and, occasionally, the basest of thieves. From somewhere at the top of the building, the night would burst alive with drums beating strange rhythms that tempted him. Voices would sing, bottles would crack, and men would curse. This, he knew, should not worry him. It was only the voices of the good men and women turned drunk in the refuge of the night brothel after a hard day's work. It was also the turn of pimps and whores galore to smile their way into the good men's pockets after a hard day's rest, scratching one another's faces in the process.

He never knew why they were considered so bad. The good men and women woke up when the sun's warm rays pushed out of his back lane the reluctant cold of dawn. The whores and pimps went to their own beds then, so what? In a way he thought of the men with that curious envy of the ignorant. He remembered having once asked his brother how old he was. He had been told "fourteen." For all he knew, Mbane could be much older. He could not tell — did it matter? But his brother must have been married around his own age. And yet he himself would never be able to reach out his hand in fulfilment of his life in the same way.

He could only yearn impotently beyond the reach of darkness and lameness. At such times when bitter self-pity overcame him, he thought of his own light and then he would smile broadly and bravely.

"Take this medicine." It was his brother's wife, Sarah, breaking into the hut. Slowly and tenderly she raised his head and put the cup to his mouth. The bitter fluid explored down his throat and another attack of pain tore through his stomach.

"You will be all right soon," Sarah said. "God will be good to you."

He knew she did not hold out much hope for him. She withdrew after laying him on the bed to which he had tried to accustom himself since being "rescued" from the hard pavement. Heavier footsteps told him that his brother, Ezekiel, had come in. He sat on his bed. No one spoke for a long time. He himself could not be expected to start a conversation. All his life he had been speaking to himself in his thoughts, and for a long time on the street, except for his mechanical plea of "Yes?", he had no one to address but himself. Now, if anyone spoke to him, he could only carry the subject on a line of uncommunicative thought in his own mind.

"Mbane, do you believe in God?" Ezekiel asked.

He saw no reason why his brother should ask him this. He only answered to himself, "I don't know. I don't think it matters."

He remembered their religious mother who was now long dead. She used to say that all men were one stream, one flow through the rocks of life. Twisting and turning the pebbles, they would get dirty in the muddy earth. They cried in the falls and whirlpools of life, laughed and sang when the flow was smooth and undisturbed. And while some cried and whirled in the pot-holes of life's valley, others laughed triumph elsewhere. But it seemed to Mbane that he was not only crying. He was not even a part of that stream whose waters branched out into a narrow valley towards the heavenly pool. He was not even flowing down the wide gulf into the eternal deluge and chaos of Satan's burning sea. No, he was like the bitter liquid in his own throat, not the good water. He saw no reason why he should believe in God.

"God gives us everything," he had often heard. But did he? "God is white cleanliness, eternal light." But what was that cleanliness? What did light mean to a blind man? Did not his life contain a darkness, a blackness no one would understand? Did the Christmas morning procession of good men and women in the City mean anything more to him than that the generous in yesterday's mean men would be evoked, meaning more money for his hat? As they sang and whistled the carol and hallelujah down the morning street; as they got drunk and cursed at one another earlier than usual, he felt he did not belong, and they had forgotten him. But had they ever remembered or ever actually noticed him? True they would pray for him as a matter of course, and drop him a coin. But instead of bringing the knowledge of Christ to him, much as he wished that he should be left alone, some good Christian men and women would once again curse, call him able-bodied, only crippled more every day by the idleness of leisurely begging.

He could tell this, too, in the way the authority in the City handled him. It sometimes surprised him that the big vehicle which emptied the dustbin had never swept him away in the raucous noise. And yet, Mbane was convinced, it was a glorious thing to believe, to cling, to dream of a future life. It was glorious this feeling, that far, far away beyond the pangs of darkness lay light, bigger and more meaningful than that which his eyes were denied. There someone would understand and raise the innocence of his crippled life along with the chosen. It gave him hope, and he sang his own happy song, silently to himself, secretly. To the passer-by let his face appear discernible. Yet this happy thought filled his time. It was his refuge at night too, as they found theirs in the brothel above him. His soul, like the letters which they dropped in the pillar box which he sometimes made the mistake of leaning against, had a destination. Often as he sat there on the pavement, he wished for his journey's end. He wished that his soul were free, flowing everywhere and not incarcerated in a body which smelt of sweat, unwashed except in rain, and which he could but feel.

"Mbane, I asked do you believe in God?" It was Ezekiel again.

"And I said I don't know," he answered weakly.

"No, you did not. You only lay there sobbing."

He lay there, knowing another attack was coming.

"Mbane — I — I want Christ to save you. Do you know where sinners go when they die, do you know where those who are saved go? There was once a man called Jes..."

"Yes, I know," Mbane swallowed painfully. "That is why you brought me here."

"And do you accept him?"

"I do not know. But I now *see* the light I have often thought about in my own way."

"You are worse than Judas!" Ezekiel hissed in suppressed anger. "Will you never stop thinking about your god even in your dy—, in this hour? I want you to be baptised."

He had become more calm now, and he smiled distantly. Ezekiel saw it was hopeless to go on. Still, he would never give his brother to the devil.

"Mbane, will you not follow the way of good men and women?"

His strength waned fast. There was no pain, only weakness. Then his head jerked down to the bed.

Ezekiel bent down and touched the cold forehead with a shaking hand.

"He is gone," he said aloud to himself.

"Yes, he is gone," Sarah whispered.

"And — he was smiling," he said, looking round at his wife.

"Yes, he was smiling."

two

it's a dog's share in our kinshasa

I always thought until that Saturday morning that I was not a sadistic man. I admit that I would have preferred a cup of hot coffee in bed to the sight of blood. But that morning I woke up earlier than usual. Everybody woke up earlier than usual. The whole town woke up earlier than usual.

There must have been something strange in the air that urged everyone to go and have their grisly worth of this very public affair at the ungainly hour of half-past six. The dawn sun crept its claws through my bedroom curtains and a sinister warmth seemed to beckon me outside. Much as I admit I am partial to the morning sun, I felt a strong urge to bury my ignorance — of what I might perhaps be capable of — in the dark comfort of the white bedsheets; and not to expose what might turn out to be self-revelation, self-betrayal. I would hate to enjoy it all.

But come to think of it, what was wrong with following the mob? What was wrong with joining in the spirit of the State? Did not the damned man deserve death?

I dressed up and hurried outside.

As I approached the execution spot a mile away, I could not help detecting a heaviness in the air. Once or twice I caught myself heaving my shoulders, like a ridiculous elephant, as if to relax.

"Traitor, traitor!" yelled the mob. The morning was clear; the issue was clear. Everything seemed — yes, seemed — in order, organised, academic. There was hardly a speck of cloud to mar the light-hearted heavens. All around was the spirited cry in chorus, *Traitor! Traitor!*

Only the air hung heavy.

Here and there were mixed faces. Black, white, brown, humanity breakfasting in unison and all pushing forward, necks craned with a strange passion. Sleepy soldiers kept us at bay. We clung to the circumference of the semi-circular rope, our limit, so that to the heavens looking down upon us, we must have appeared like a ridiculous half-moon of mad passion yawning its wide mouth, dying to send a man to his death. I remembered that to our forefathers — very superstitious, I hear — a certain shape of the moon spelt lunacy on earth.

"Great sight, eh! Hang all traitors!" said the jubilant man beside me, stretching an elastic snarl to reveal yellow teeth. Twisting his face, he scratched at the night's growth of beard. "Ever seen such a large crowd before? Funny thing is. . . hey, what's the matter with you? Friend of yours?"

No, I said, no friend of mine. I apologised for not being a great talker in the morning. But my new friend, obviously disappointed in me, muttered something like 'sentimental bitch' and turned the other way. I heard him growl and snarl what must have been the same piece of thirsty information to the man behind him. The latter on grinning back a rusty row of molars, gripped his new friend by the shoulder and barking at the top of his voice, agreed it was a spectacular sight.

Traitor! Traitor! roared the crowd, as if in echo. A peculiar oneness.

Over at the raised ground, I could just make out the features of the damned man tied to a pole. Although the raised ground was little higher than our vantage point, (our half-moon of greed being to his east), the condemned man braved the rising sun and played down at us a contemptuous grin. The smile disarmed and annoyed me. It was as if he would break loose at any moment, spring upon us like a master on his dog, and I wished I was back in bed. But as I accidentally caught sight of my unshaven companion I could have sworn he bared his teeth right back at the prisoner and I felt a strange assurance that if that contemptible man should break upon us, I was well protected. I hated that playfulness of smile because it belittled me. Did he not realise his condition? Must he look down upon us as if we were a breed of hounds?

It was now well past eight o'clock and we began to wonder. The firing squad was not yet here. Only the policemen and soldiers, who had now united forces with a rare friendliness, saw to it that we kept to the right side of the tantalising rope. As the sun rose higher and higher we began to sweat; tempers rose, cries of *Traitor! Traitor!* became more violent, and hunger stung at our bellies. The condemned man seemed to smile with contemptuous satisfaction more than ever. Perhaps the firing squad aimed to work us into this heat so that when it arrived everything would be a climax; the town gossip for weeks on end.

A clear African sunrise is no guarantee of a cloudless day. This was true of that Saturday morning. Here and there were now formed strips of clouds. But they were no umbrella against this sun which acted like a catalyst of anger, a curious inspiration. Paradoxically, it was as if we did not need any clouds at all. They seemed to disturb the orderly geometry of the heavens. Occasionally we would be questioned with a silent shadow of doubt as a cloud, on its way to the anticlimax in the west, hovered above us, obscuring the sun.

But it had now become an angry affair. Reason as to why the man was dying had fled us in our thirst for blood and we gave ourselves the benefit of this doubt.

"*Traitor! Traitor!*" cried the mob in singsong.

"Icecream!" cried a vendor.

"Coca Cola!" cried another. Business and pickpocketing flourished.

My unshaven neighbour, who now seemed to change his opinion of me for the better, swept his paw across his face to wipe off the sweat and belched a guffaw — more like the choke of a bone. He and I shared an ice-cream.

At last, about midday, the policemen and soldiers fell upon us with a physical request to make way and I now counted the firing squad of twelve cutting its way sharply into our mad crescent.

"Attention!" yelped the officer in charge. Blood rose.

For about ten minutes we seemed to be deliberately tantalised. We were the anxious spectators pressed together for the climax, or was it comfort?

Then, somewhere — in our midst — a little girl cried. Diving under the rope, she ran towards the officer with a bunch of flowers. A soldier intercepted her. But the officer noticed and said in his stiff posture, sword up, that the girl could come to him — or something like that, I was too far to hear. After a still minute or so, the little girl hesitated her way to the doomed man and at last stood looking up at his heroic face. He did not so much as look down. He had, it appeared, worked himself into a trance. When he did finally notice the girl — the flowers — his contemptuous smile vanished. He was, apparently, moved. It seemed to us that he asked the little girl to put the flowers at his feet. For the first time he had dropped his head and, although I was too far to see clearly, I had no doubt that the smile had been but a veneer, a screen against our hardness of heart; and he wept. With gratitude? Grief? I don't know. All I can say is that as the little girl wept her way back again, a knowledge of something sacred betrayed to public emotion seemed to have touched our hearts and weighed there heavily, like the day of judgement.

Women drew out their handkerchiefs. We, the brave men, seemed to drop our heads down in chorus and pressed together. With shame? Even that I cannot tell. But I found myself moving away — backing out? — towards home, tail between my legs.

Behind me, I saw the unshaven man he, too, bent on all fours, beaten. He made an attempt to address me but suspecting, rightly, that I would not answer him, scratched at his itchy beard and thought the better of it. The whole thing was itchy. Maybe he too could not wait for the climax. Maybe he too had been touched at a very soft spot. But we had not far to escape. We heard the report of shots and turned in time to take our due share of the violent anticlimax. The next we knew we had clutched at each other.

This is what we had come for: smoke at one end, blood and dust at the other.

We disengaged ourselves, rather ridiculously I must say, and he went a different way; for a strengthening lunch, no doubt.

three

god's water

The rain was welcomed with much rejoicing. The crying earth drank it deep and its cracks were healed. New cracks formed when for a short while the mud hardened, but they were beautiful fresh cracks and they disappeared with the next torrent. The dust seemed forever gone.

During drought it had discoloured the white clay of the huts. The embittered rain now struck at these walls in a blind rage and ate away the dust and the white clay and into the brown, hard mud. Sometimes it ate right through and the occupants of the huts were unpleasantly aware of a cold wind searching through their persons.

The children loved the rain. Outside the houses the ground was slippery. They ran and let their feet slide as far as possible, keeping balance with their outstretched arms. Sometimes they fell and rolled in the mud. The women sat on stools near the doorway, winnowing a little maize and watching them with a smile. It gave them pleasure to see their children so full of life. And they were lively too. The heat that had sapped their strength was gone, God be praised.

During the drought the maize and beans had shrivelled up. Food was dear in the market. The sun had been bitter as they came home carrying their bags on their backs. Their hearts had cried and the cracked earth had cried with them. Bellies had pricked and gnawed.

They were still pricking and gnawing, for the ground had just gulped the new seed, but there was a new song in the air. The hopeless silence was gone. Nature had drunk in health and had stirred.

The rain went on for weeks, beating down violently. At first there was only joy. In the Church the voices soared high in praise to God Almighty. The preacher was triumphant as he read: "Ye of little Faith..." He knew their hearts had weakened during the drought although he had urged them to be strong in their faith and pray.

"Ye of little Faith..."

Then news came of floods. Homes had been destroyed and crops washed away. The crops along the bend of the Thiria River, which had suffered little during the drought were covered by water. Brown, forbidding water.

One morning as he drove to Church the preacher was shaken to find that the Thiria bridge had been washed away. The bridge had been built in 1954. Before then there had been two precarious logs across the river. In that year the Government decided to construct a wooden bridge so that Government vehicles could pass through the route as they went to fight the Mau Mau in the northern parts of the district. But that first version had been lost in fierce flames lit by a rebellious hand. The new Thiria bridge, whose skeleton now lay in bits somewhere in the depths of the river, had been constructed in the following year. Its disappearance was a great shock to the preacher. He sat behind the wheel of an old Volkswagen staring at the swollen waters. He had based his text on Hebrew 13:15, "Let us offer the sacrifice to God continually, giving thanks to his name." But in the face of this new crisis he could only think of the words: "And God said unto Noah, 'Make thee an Ark.' " And that would be his text.

After the sermon a solemn, highly moved crowd gathered outside the Church to discuss the floods. They talked excitedly about the bridge.

"We have seen nothing," said a stocky gentleman, with an air of one with wide knowledge of current affairs. "We have seen nothing. The Wakambas' crops have all been destroyed. Their homes have been washed away. America is flying food to them in planes."

"My vegetables in the valley — they are covered in water," said a sad-eyed, long-suffering woman. She was giving the plain facts not seeking pity. God worked in mysterious ways his wonders to perform, and who was she to question that which He had ordained?

"So are my arrow-roots," said another. "You cannot see them now. You cannot see anything. I saw a few leaves..."

"You have seen nothing," said the informed gentleman. "You have seen nothing, daughter of our Father. Believe me. Do you read *Taifa?*"

The woman stared at him. She could not read the Lord's words.

The gentleman nodded triumphantly.

"You should read *Taifa,*" he said. His manner suggested that he could not even attempt to *outline* the fantastic things that were happening all around them. To understand them with any lucidity, one had to read *Taifa* . He was not excited about the bridge being swept away or a few arrow-roots being covered by water. He knew the plight of other people in other districts.

"You should listen to the radio," he concluded.

"I know not what we shall drink," said a woman; revealing the sore that now throbbed in her life. "The water is very very bad. It is not *good* for drinking."

She lived in a mud hut roofed with grass. Her problem was plain and was widely shared. Those whose homes had corrugated iron roofs were detachedly sympathetic. Round the edges of their roofs was a drain directing water into drums. It was cold, clear water straight from God.

But you cannot drain a grass roof. The rain loses itself in the grass and some trickles out slowly, tainted with smoke. When the grass warms with the sun, the roofs smoke as the water ascends back into the clouds.

The woman and the others who, like her, used grass for their roofs, depended on the water from the river. It was a long time since there was so much of it, but who knew what else, besides the bridge, it had washed along? The woman, who was a clean woman, feared disease. She was strongly against the Thiria water.

"A person may die," she revealed to the sympathetic crowd.

* * *

Njoki, wife of Mugane, was ready to assist those grass roofers who came to her for help. A year before, as though from a premonition of the drought, her husband had tapped the subterranean water. All through the dry months, the pulse of the pump had faithfully sustained life on the farm. Her husband had bought yards of hose pipe. The pastures and her husband's vegetables were preserved by veins from the pump. Now the pump was still as the rain poured. There was more water than was needed. It was surprising to see others in need and she did not hesitate to help them.

Stephen Mugane saw strange women around the farm. At first he thought nothing of it. There were always strange women working on the farm. Then he realised what was happening and he summoned his wife.

"It appears you are giving water to women," he said.

She hesitated. She could smell trouble. She knew he did not approve.

"Yes," she said.

"And why should you give them water?"

Her reply was quick. She understood the women's problems and she tried to explain them to him. But she knew he would not understand.

"If the water from the river is dirty, they should boil it," he said, cutting her short. "There is . . ."

"Boil it! It takes so long to boil a pot of water. Why should they go to all that trouble when we have so much water to spare?".

He was angry. She had interrupted him. And she had led him into an argument.

"I say they must boil it," he flared. "Or drink it like that. What did they do when there were no pumps, eh? Why do they suddenly turn away from the river water? What did you do when you did not have a pump? And were you not brought up with water from the river? I say I don't want strange women here asking for water. Get rid of them."

That was that. She left his presence with a heavy heart.

She stared unseeingly before her as she stood in the kitchen. She was wondering how she would tell the women when they came the next time for water. This was the sort of thing that was sure to earn the family a bad name. When she went to church the following Sunday, she knew someone would throw a remark about the matter.

She stood by the kitchen window while she waited for some water to heat up, and she looked down the coffee-flanked driveway that joined the road. The bleak vastness of the sky with its drizzle seemed to depress her further and dark thoughts gathered in her mind. And she feared lest a stooping, blanket-clad figure should make its appearance at that inopportune moment and place her in the depths of embarrassment before she was well braced for it.

But it was also usual at this time that the restless sea of maternal anxiety should rise within her, and she would be held there at the window watching for her little daughter. There had been a time — now distant and irretrievable — when the big house had rung and echoed with the laughter of all her children and buzzed with their activity. But two of them were now married and only came for an occasional visit, while the other two were lodged in distant boarding schools which disgorged them into her arms for brief spells only to wrench them away again.

Like a spirit breathed forth by the coffee trees, a small girl in a green uniform made an appearance at the end of the driveway and came towards the house. Njoki's vigil ended in peace, she turned from the window and gave heed to the pot now grumbling and fuming on the electric cooker. She threw in some tea leaves as if to appease it. Soon the awaited clatter of young feet and the scraping of mud on the scraper outside came to her ears. The door opened and the room admitted the little girl, clutching some dog-eared books. She was a little wet and small drops like crystals hung in her hair.

Njoki turned and surveyed her daughter.

"You are not too wet," she said. "But is it cold outside?"

"Wee-che!" said the little girl and she shivered.

"Very cold?" Njoki said with a smile. "You will not catch a cold. You had your little coat on."

She smoothed back the girl's hair, flaking off the watery crystals. She was a very pretty girl with fine delicate features that closely resembled her mother's. Njoki had a fierce, possessive love for this child, her last born.

"Go and change, mother's child," she told her and watched her walk into the corridor that led to the bedrooms. They met in that corridor as the girl came back in a rather tight, yellow dress and as she herself was going to take a pot of tea to her husband.

"Pour out a cup of tea for yourself," Njoki told her. "And see that you do not burn yourself."

"Who is that for?"

"Your father."

"He is going away."

"Going away?"

And outside there was the sound of the car to confirm the girl's words. The engine roared as it warmed up. Then it purred as Stephen left home.

* * *

During the drought the roads had been steeped in dust, soft fine dust that baked the people's feet. It was gritty in their mouths where the wind blew it. The cars had been autocratic on the roads and the people had fled to the hedges when they sped past, trailing a cloud of dust. Pressed against the hedges, pedestrians would wait in patience for the dust to clear a little. Their hair and eyelashes wore a yellow film of it.

But the mud now lay like thick porridge on the roads. The cars wearily crawled along in a zig-zag motion, and their wheels lapped it up and revelled in it. Then the wheels could take no more. The cars ground to a giddy halt. . .

* * *

From the kitchen window Njoki and her daughter could see, beyond the green sea of the coffee, the china-coloured top of the car. They could hear its roar, angry but hushed by the distance. And soon there was activity, evident in the flitting of a head or two, and then the slow, strained tortoise movement of the car.

"They are pushing it," said the little girl. She was suddenly eager with excitement. "Mother, shall I go?"

"Go where?"

"To help Father."

"No, stay here," Njoki told her. In her heart there was, as she watched the half-obscured activity on the road, the conflicting feelings of a wife who would wish her husband to get unstuck, and at the same time hope that he might stick at home. And so her relief mingled strangely with an empty dissatisfaction as she watched the car crawl at last and disappear from her vision.

She remained there at the window, but her mind was far away. Perhaps her mind strained to follow him through paths she had never trodden. Hers had ever been a small world and he moved in circles she had only vague notions of, for she had never had a foothold from which to explore it. It was a world that was about her as she stood besieged in her own; a world that clamoured about her so near yet so remote. He rode the paths he fancied and she, sensing that he strayed, grieved in silence.

She did not notice the little girl, for whom the drama had closed, walk away towards her bedroom to seek fresh interests.

Then there appeared, coming down the driveway, a familiar figure of a woman. At the sight of her Njoki shrunk a little. Her mind was at once confused and she groped for things to say.

The woman came up and tapped on the kitchen door. Njoki opened it, a strained smile curving her lips. The woman was smiling broadly as if determined to display what remained of her set of teeth.

"Such funny things," she said as she relieved herself of the water vessel on her back. She threw back her head and her ribs shook with ripples of laughter. "Your husband, Njoki. He is a funny one. 'Heave, old woman, heave!' " she cried, and shrieked with laughter. "I tell you I could not heave. He kept on saying 'Heeeve...!' like a warrior going into battle. I just rocked with laughter and he heaved alone. And he is *such* a strong man!"

There was a pause punctuated by her bubbles of laughter.

Njoki said, "Come in and have some tea. The weather is so cold..."

"It will be late shortly," said the woman, "and my son has lost his key. Such a careless boy you have never seen. Now he cannot enter the house without me about. No, Njoki, thank you. I will only fill up this vessel and then I will be gone."

"No, come in," Njoki said in unusually firm tone. "I will not take too much of your time."

four

the stranger

He just happened. None of us knew where he came from, how long he would stay and — if he would after all carry his suspect self away — where he was bound. He just happened. And the next we knew he had planted his small tent in our midst without the slightest inclination to ceremonies. He seemed to be one of those inarticulate figures who would assert themselves without a word — only a grunt, perhaps — and get away with it.

He was in fact crude, and very rude.

That is how we had to dismiss this man whom we could not pin down to a label, either of tribe or origin; this arrogant piece of work which carried no identity card — and got away with it. For those were for us the hard days of the Emergency when you could not afford to move where you liked without the Government's neat documents. Every house had a number and every man of over sixteen carried a blue identity card which he would have liked to throw away, yet dared not. For while it signified his curtailed freedom, to be found without it meant certain arrest; and whether subsequent deportation to Manyani Detention Camp followed depended very much on whether the homeguards liked his face or not. Alternatively, a man could always bribe his way out, or speak English provided one did not look as if one was trying to impress the uneducated homeguards, who would in that case strike harder than ever. With Her Majesty's rifle in his hand, a homeguard was very rarely impressed by a black face. Matters became worse if you were a stranger. For the least one could do was to drop a few names one knew in the homeguard's ear, promptly naming your host and his house number. Now and then you could tell a good lie (in fact there was little room for honesty) and manage to fool the homeguard, who after all may be new and unlikely to know everybody.

They are still very hazy in my mind, those days. It was as if a cloud had suddenly fallen upon our old homes when one Sunday morning the headman of our sub-location ordered every man, woman and child to congregate at the homeguard post. He had announced on behalf of 'my friend District Officer Robinson', on behalf of the Provincial Commissioner, on behalf of Justice, Law and Order, on behalf of Her Majesty's Government which stood no nonsense and on behalf of God-knows-who-else that we had exactly five weeks to vacate our homes. We were to build a big village on the slopes of a mild hill where it would be 'strategic for the government to bomb all simultaneously if you don't behave.' Also, the headman went on, this way we would be well protected both from one another and from the Mau Mau terrorists in which case we were 'not to worry'. We would be well taken care of in the neat rows of houses which were to be of mud, wood, thatch-roof or corrugated iron according to one's degree of affluence, or according to how much some people had been robbing others over the years.

Waving a large sheet, he stamped his shoes and swore that the order had been signed personally by the District Commissioner. (We children had sat nearest the headman's platform while the adults stood gathered behind us obediently like the Lord's sheep. I could just make out the neat, admirable scrawl which the headman said was the D.C.'s very own signature 'as I am sure I am standing here'. It waved solemnly across the bottom of the large sheet like the tail of gunsmoke in a cowboy cartoon, and we children were impressed.) But if we thought that that was all the message we were mistaken. For it also said that a police siren would now scuttle through the new village to announce the curfew at five minutes to six o'clock, in time for a lorry-load of homeguards to follow at five minutes past six and shoot like a dog anyone on sight. In this respect too, we were given three weeks to strangle our dogs which were certain to defecate our new, neat village, and whose one canine ambition was to bite 'my friend D.O. Robinson.' (If we did not stone them to death, he said, the homeguards would collect any stray dog and take it to the Rifle-range where they would practise markmanship on it. After which the owner was to bury the carcass and pay five shillings for each of all those wasted bullets.)

It might be hard on those who owned cattle and goats too. One couldn't eat all that meat in five weeks. So those animals, the headman went on, could be left on our farms to be stolen by the terrorists and homeguards alike. One could, however, keep a cow or two on one's new plot, which measured one-eighth of an acre, for the purpose of milk. Also, he would not particularly object to our keeping hens, although they must not stray. (He need hardly have said this. He was a frequent visitor to certain houses where he tickled the breasts of the deserted wives — thus excusing them from compulsory communal labour — and was known to be partial to chicken, like 'my friend D. O. Robinson' to whom he occasionally made a present of the eggs.)

The headman then summoned the village preacher and told him to lead the prayers.

Thus, after five weeks, we fell into the neat rows. Most people filled in the mud-wall while already occupying the house during the night. The poles would stand naked and jagged, pointing heavenwards in all kinds of ungainly ways like bare legs. I suppose being 'shot on sight' did not apply for the first three weeks. You could still see families huddled around the fire under a scanty roof. Occasionally a home-guard would run after a stray dog at night and, his nostrils alert, find that he had himself strayed into the house with the best food.

Whatever else a man did to make himself and his family comfortable, the thing to remember was to fix a door as soon as the poles were erect so that the government sign-writer could paint a neat number on the door, thus completing the man's credentials. Our fathers' lives had in fact become incomplete without numbers:

'Joram Ngige? Your house number? Identity card number? Number of wives? Number of children? Other dependants? And I suppose you have taken oath number seven? Number of previous convictions? Number of bullets caught on you? ...'

Then, when they all had numbers, he happened. He just occurred.

I suppose I can claim the distinction of having discovered the stranger. I had woken up at about six o'clock on a Saturday morning, the earliest hour that my elder sister

Wangeci would have dared send me anywhere for the curfew did not end until then. Everybody was asleep and I could hear my father snoring as dawn crept into my room through a dozen ready cracks. I sat up playing a ray in the palm of my hand.

"Up! Up!" It was my beautiful sister Wangeci. She taught at the village primary school where she settled all her domestic accounts with me without any visible discrimination as to blood as she spanked me along with other culprits. Now she stormed into my room and said, "Up! Up, you lazy pup! Go and get me soap — same as always."

That phrase 'same as always' was driving me mad. It referred to Lux toilet soap which Wangeci always used since it was recommended by some of the world's most beautiful women including nine out of ten film stars.

I opened the window. The day felt somewhat strange as I had not really become used to the new life. But the sun felt equally warm and easy, and nostalgic, as the easy breeze flapped my large, loose shirt. (Although I had graduated into a pair of shorts, I found them cumbersome off-school and rarely wore them especially since Wangeci insisted I should). In the old days we children would have spent the Saturday playing or herding cattle in the valley. But tension had now swept us too along with our parents. The frequent sounds of machine guns down the valley, which had been for us innocent but now loomed large with danger as men died, did not help. Each stayed with his own, distrusted other children and their parents particularly, and avoided strangers. We had matured into the puberty of distrust sometime before we could boast the years.

I left the house and struck out up the government's impressive road towards the shop. I was in no particular hurry. Beautiful women could wait. Somehow I didn't quite understand Wangeci. My mother, who had died at my birth, had apparently won my father's heart with a saying which went something like, 'What is a beautiful face without a beautiful soul to match?' It may not have been original and as I went to the shop now it hung stale on my ears like some of those regular clichés the Sunday school teacher dished out to keep up morale. But my father, who was blessed with two very dowry-worthy daughters, if one wayward son who would amount to little in life anyhow, had nevertheless been impressed. He drummed the saying into my beautiful sisters. Their mother, he admonished, had had one of the most beautiful faces, minds, and the kindest of hearts to match. And she didn't have to read *Woman Fair* to follow the latest developments in soap-suds. But Wangeci read *Woman Fair*. She continued to be less like a mother I never knew and for whose death she no doubt resented me. I had the feeling that we might ripen her up for some young man with education but we would be lucky if we eventually milked any dowry from the clean-shaven youth.

One of the young men who nursed dreams about Wangeci was in fact the village preacher himself. He owned the shop I was now going to. But while one might expect that Kanyua would make friends by giving me a small biscuit here and a small toffee there so that I might speak well of him to Wangeci, he saved the cents like a true shopkeeper. Of course he may have done this on purpose, knowing very well that this is what I expected. He knew that Wangeci did not like him and perhaps I might not help much anyway. He preached powerfully on Sundays but had been known by my father to have conspired with the headman about my father's daughter on a weekday. The idea was to blackmail her by saying my father would be arrested on some charge or other unless she promised to marry the preacher. (It was not necessary to lay a definite charge against him as an individual. For, collectively, a Kikuyu was already guilty: organising oath-taking ceremonies, covering terrorists, conspiring to instigate country-wide strikes, forging papers, eating human flesh not least of all lost homeguards, manufacturing guns, and the like. It was, simply, a question of pin-pointing any of these to the cheeky individual who might perhaps only be late for curfew or communal labour. So that in those days of 'intense mechanisation' where lives were reduced to the science of guns and numbers, prisoners were never certain what particular charge would take the whims of the homeguards at any given moment. These charges could be as ridiculous and amusing as they were often tragic. But my father did not wait to be summoned. He believed in drawing the arrows first, especially since gossip tellers never substantiated their hearsay. One simply grew long rabbit-ears to weigh the rumours in the wind, then waited for the government to come and torture him or the terrorists to come for his head: or decided to take the risk and react violently like my father. For my old man had little patience. Like a big man, he summoned the preacher and the headman to our house, which took them a little off their guard, no doubt. Then he told the young preacher to come off the pulpit and uncloak himself. The conspiracy was over. The headman asked for a glass of water. My father told him to go to the river. The headman again rose up gallantly to the occasion and said something like, Don't you see the Right Reverend likes the soil Wangeci trots on? But my father didn't like the way these two men trod the ground in their shuffling boots. Although he was thought to be a 'good' Christian — in fact the headman seemed to respect him for this — in reality he regarded the Church and the government with equal contempt. Often — quietly in the house, for walls had ears — he said that the reverend was the most perfect shopkeeper in the country. My father's friends seemed to have either been scattered by the government and the terrorists or no longer trusted us for they never came to our house now. So, lately, he seemed to expect in me an adult confidant whenever he condemned the 'self-righteous Church', the white soldiers on holiday from school who lost their virginity by raping the daughters of the land 'on behalf of the government'; and the impotent sons of the land who he claimed had lost the common, virile vision and were now slaughtering their own people aimlessly like a tribe or tired sadists. I couldn't help feeling that he and I were in turn organising our own little conspiracy of self-righteousness which would alienate and isolate us, whereas we had in fact no right to think ourselves better than anyone else. But I never talked back to my father. Nevertheless I found it almost amusing now for the preacher seemed to approach him as one man of God to another. He disarmed them, however, with a short sermon on morality as he held me by the shirt and referred the preacher to some chapter in the bible. Then he stamped his boots and scared them.)

Kanyua often interpreted the Bible in a remarkably contradictory fashion to accommodate his whims. His only predictable saying as far as I can remember was that one could not be precise about the soul because Jesus spoke in parables, and the Old Testament being in fact an old testament of the Jews by the Jews and for the Jews should be forgotten. I didn't trust him.

I made for his shop now, sweeping my bare feet on the dew which glittered on the grass at the side of the road. An early, no doubt stray, dog which must have escaped being shot barked at me, then followed. Apart from a few workers who had to catch the early bus to Nairobi I met no one. The village was usually peaceful at this early hour. Then, as I approached Kanyua's shop at the centre of the village where it rubbed shoulders with the Government's high tower, I stopped suddenly. There, on the other side of Kanyua's shop, an old army tent had been put up rather carelessly and as if the owner had erected it the previous night without a light to see by, or as if he had been in a hurry to go to sleep. It fluttered in the cool breeze with an air of utter detachment. I said 'Jimmy!' to the dog as it barked towards the tent and the dog, which needed no formal christening, ran by my side as if to acknowledge gratefully that 'Jimmy!' would do. We moved away from the tent. Perhaps it was just another crank who wanted to bring trouble to our village. If so he had better know we already had enough trouble in our village. Jimmy and I went into the shop.

"Lux toilet soap," I said.

Padre Kanyua's youngest brother Mwangi (a snob about my age but who wore shorts to impress the rest of us) was dozing behind the counter. He now sprang to life but, seeing it was only me, dug an impressive cartoon book from under the counter and started reading. I wished the young scholar a good day and told him to give me the soap, same as always.

"You should read this too," said the scholar. "It's good for *us*". He was laughing.

But before I had said what I thought about Saturday morning scholars, Reverend Kanyua emerged immaculate from behind the curtain which separated the shop from the living rooms. He didn't ask for any money because my father always settled his accounts at the end of the month.

"Sixty five shillings ninety-two cents this month," said the Reverend. The scholar wrote it down in the accounts book.

"Nine out of ten film stars," he was saying. This was clearly rude.

"Education!" I said. Jimmy barked.

"Shs. . . . . .h!" hushed the reverend, ushering me out.

Again I stopped by the army tent. No self-respecting army man would have pitched his tent so carelessly. I went over and peeped inside. Jimmy barked again. A heap of dark clothes sprung up and a hand flung a hammer at Jimmy who barked even louder.

Then, utterly indifferent, the ragged man came out of the tent. He was an old man, slightly bent, and as he flung us a look it was if he was staring beyond us into the distance, as if in fact we could not hope to be the object of his immediate concern. He brought out a small stool and sat on it for a moment; his hands on his knees, eyes staring up the Government's straight road which disappeared into the horizon. Then he withdrew into the tent and almost immediately came out with a small tool box and a dirty cotton sack.

He held the sack upside down and an assortment of shoes and boots came tumbling out in an ungainly fashion and piled up dirtily like a heap of rubbish, waiting to be burnt clean into consummation. I stood there, fascinated. But the stranger was not burning anything. He was only a shoemaker, he seemed to say as he gave me a glance, and his business was to mend. He put a shoe on a last which was battered but no doubt still useful, ready for yet another broken sole.

Then he took the hammer and beat at the heel methodically. The metallic thud which died on the last like the unimpressive sound of a gun with a silencer reached the impeccable doors of the padre's shop and brought out the scholar.

Mwangi was appalled. He retreated immediately into the shop and brought out Reverend Kanyua. Kanyua was scandalised.

But the shoemaker gave Kanyua one unaffected look which pierced beyond the horizon and drove in another nail. Then he swept his eyes over our feet and shook his head. Clearly, his business was shoes. He did not say a word. He took another look at my bare feet. They were all but covered by my large american-khaki shirt. A blade of wet grass was caught here and there in between the toes which shot out unimpressively from under the shirt. For the first time I took an interest in my feet. The big toe on the right and stronger foot looked particularly ugly with its dented nail. The shoemaker shook his head. The scholar, who wore thick shoes, clacked his heels and hitched the belt of his shorts into position. Loudly clicked the buckles. He held his book so that the front cover was folded with half the leaves onto the back cover to display his progress with the cowboys since my departure five minutes ago.

"Who's this?" the reverend demanded, and stamped his polished boots.

The shoemaker beat in another nail. It was by this time apparent that he was a stranger, unknown, unwelcome. And in those days one could not move where one liked, camp in other people's — our — village and make no attempt whatsoever to present one's credentials. It was both suspect and very rude. One had to have a label and identify oneself immediately with somebody, or something, at least.

The reverend was now extremely irritated. How could this audacious character who looked so shabby and so arrogantly detached put up a tent on his very own plot? He, Reverend Kanyua, famous young preacher of the location, would soon fix this old Undesirable.

"Must be evil," said the reverend and left.

"Ought to be shot by a cowboy," said the scholar and stamped the ground after his elder brother to the tower.

I stood there fascinated. The shoemaker grinned at me to welcome a conspirator and raised the hammer towards the disappearing legs, as the brothers made for the homeguard tower. Their path seemed broken and they shuffled their polished shoes in a series of jigging hops that would have embarrassed anybody but themselves. I, too, could hardly restrain a laugh. Jimmy fell in conspiratorially by the shoemaker's side like an old friend. I watched the morning caress those two and I felt there was perhaps more to the stranger than the reverend and the cowboy had cared to read beyond the mere fact of a trespass. He looked at me again and made some noise. For the first time I realised he was dumb.

Presently, the homeguard came. He held a baton in his hand and his starched khaki shorts were creased sharp. He looked knives at the shoemaker, caressing the only chevron up his left sleeve with an enthusiasm which betrayed that the chevron had been newly presented.

"Move!" was his first word. "Where is your identity card?"

The shoemaker drove in yet another nail.

"Hey! Have you the ears to hear?" said Reverend Kanyua.

Another nail. The methodic uninterrupted clang of the hammer. Over there, in the distance, a late cock crows and villagers open their windows to greet the day. Over here irritated feet shuffle uneasily.

"Satan's work is always suspect," says the padre. The scholar reads another page of the cowboys in one glance and shuts his book with a loud noise.

After a few moments the guard says, "I am going for the headman!" This is clearly becoming difficult.

"What's it all about?" says the padre who had expected the guard to handle the trespasser all by himself.

* *

The homeguard post lay on the outskirts of the village. It had been built by the forced communal effort of all our loitering fathers and mothers. A deep trench ran round it. It had a net of barbed wire laid inside as well as wooden spikes which pointed in all directions ready to pounce on any mau mau who might be up to some trick. Broken bottles, nails, bones, shoes, boots, knives, bicycle parts, steering wheels, and crushed tins had been thrown in as a further deterrent. This was where the headman lived with a gay troupe of about eighty homeguards. There they made love to the deserted wives and killed chickens. One felt that while they were there to protect us, they were very well protected themselves. But the terrorists became convinced that the homeguards were in fact chicken themselves after dark, and little better than the Police who had a habit of retreating when attacked, leaving the dirty work to the King's African Rifles (KAR).

So the terrorists set the trench on fire with cans of petrol on one of those merry nights. The trench which had protected so well became a nightmare, and the homeguards would have perished were it not for a squad of the KAR which came to their rescue. Twenty men died but the headman survived, to fly for the first time in his life in a Government helicopter.

Accompanied by Reverend Kanyua, he dropped neat red leaflets and promised us 'Martial Laws' from a Government loud speaker, while the young reverend said, Let us pray for the lost souls.

This was in broad daylight and we would be relieved to see the helicopter drone away to promise the same to other villages where the culprits might be in hiding. But the pained voice would fade neatly away only to come back again and hammer down messages we often heard from less uplifted premises. Our faces were upturned as in prayer; and because the declaration of martial law had been under consideration by Her Majesty for some time and had become very real to us, we did pray secretly when the reverend requested it. One had the impression that while the reverend said, Brethren let us pray, the headman was busy surveying the land to see who had the most cattle back on his farm. In fact no one was more convinced about this than my cynical father because a week after that fifty of our cows had disappeared.

In broad daylight the homeguards became a terror to us. They whipped and threatened to circumcise us boys, running the women up and down to the river for water. The men had to show cause why they should not be sent to the Manyani Detention Camp as they mixed the water with red earth, to rebuild the walls of the homeguard post under the whip. We were all suspected of harbouring strangers. In turn, amongst ourselves, we suspected one another of giving cover to the terrorists, blaming our suffering on anyone beyond our immediate family. A conversation between old friends now became marked with the er-'s and um-h's of tense misunderstanding. Each man guarded against catches laid like a trap in the other's words and competed, subtly, to steer the wheel of conversation himself lest he be flushed down the pipeline to Manyani. And when their backs were turned each learnt to have an eye at the back of his head and warned his children against the other man's urchins.

Only when we could all turn our eyes on a stranger did we, in a generous spirit of common sadism and triumphant revenge, feel free to come together again and jointly hand the trespasser to the headman. He never thanked us. But it would be too good to last; the stranger would be locked up out of sight. The object of our collectiveness thus gone, we would break paths again to our isolated and lonely huts where we washed the dust off our feet, perhaps now individually feeling that the whole thing was a dirty conspiracy that we did not want to associate with after all. We had handed a man over 'for further questioning' — as though we had questioned him disinterestedly ourselves — because he was an outsider whose house number we could not trace among our own.

This was what I could see happening now as the padre and the scholar came marching back with the headman.

"My friend Dorobinson," said the friend of D.O. Robinson, "will not like this."

"I do not like it headman," said the preacher. "This is my very own plot Number 10."

The headman approached the shoemaker.

"Ger-up!"

* * *

Sound of the hammer. Jimmy barks, identifies himself with the stranger. I seem to have mislaid the toilet soap; this is no clean matter. Another metallic clang on the last and the reverend clacks his polished heels. The scholar oscillates between the shop where he serves the early customers, and the tense, naked situation at his doorstep where he reads another chapter. The shoemaker eventually looks round, lands his eyes on the headman's big boots, shakes his head. I, too, look at the headman's boots. We all look at the headman's boots. The friend of Dorobinson becomes self-conscious, then angry. His big boots are worn out on the outside so that the left heel particularly is eaten almost to the upper while there are still inches of the sole to the instep. The shoemaker shakes his head again at such an unreasonable and lop-sided approach to the roads of life. The headman looks round, suddenly settling his hat into position as if to assert that he is his own best chiropodist. Suspense. The metallic, steady beat. Then a crack of the whip on the shoemaker's back. He makes a sound which tears frightfully in the placid morning, something between the cry of a humiliated adult and the whining of a choked dog. He recovers, throws the hammer at the headman. The headman hides behind two of his guards, pushes them forward, says Arrest, arrest! One guard springs forward to arrest and the shoemaker spills him over his shoulder with a twist of the arm, lands him into a pile of unmended shoes. Arrest, arrest! The other guard takes his turn. But the old Undesirable who must have been hammering for a long time seems to have surprised them with his strength and the other guard is hesitant. They face each other with open arms, springing sideways, in and out, each looking for an opening.

Up to now, I have always envisaged a fight between these so-called sensible adults as an affair where the reasons for fighting are clear-cut and where each has no one to blame but himself if he gets trodden into the mud. Now as I stand here, something seems mislaid in the placid morning. The tradition of mobile film vans (which our sub-location used to look forward to, in the predictable days before the Emergency, twice a year) was that Tarzan and Charlie Chaplin may have been outnumbered but they were going to win cleanly and neatly in the end. Their adversaries — who were usually dirty for Tarzan and needed toilet soap, or immoral and with a tendency to rape for Chaplin — were dead or beaten even before they started. We all knew this and we would duly reward Tarzan in the end after two hours of laudable sadism with our loud village applause, disappointed that it had all ended without enough slaying of the blacks. "It's only a film," we would say.

But here is no loved Tarzan shaking savages from the tree, off the screen and in broad daylight. The shoemaker downs the homeguard again but he seems to say painfully that he is no hero. He appears all too human as he mutely acknowledges the admiring stares of villagers who have now crowded round to support the underdog because it is the headman, rather than they themselves, who discovered the stranger, thus denying them the benefit of their 'preliminary questioning'. The toilet soap falls out of my hand.

* * *

As soon as the shoemaker threw the second and third homeguards down I knew the headman would send for another. In fact he seemed to be enjoying himself although he had to maintain an angry face in view of the people watching. I wondered what the reverend would do if it came to his turn. Arrest, arrest! It was a dirty trick and it reminded me of my two uncles who had fought before we moved to separate plots in the village. I cannot clearly remember why they had quarrelled. But they rolled over each other on the ground, the one uncle with his hands around the other's throat making him eat and cough the soil. When their wives separated them, each hurried to his hut. Ngige, who had always bullied people like a government, came out with a bow and poisoned arrows while Kairu brought a large club and a shield to protect himself from the bully. Both were afraid of each other but swore venomously to hide the fact because their wives were there. When Kairu discovered his club was useless he fled back into the hut. The bully followed in hot pursuit only to be chased out again with a homemade gun by Kairu whose wife said that the bullied too were 'not of one cutting side like a knife'. We children bit our thumb-nails and swung our eyes from Ngige's hut to Kairu's hut, from the bully to the underdog. But then the homeguards came. Kairu was taken to Manyani as a hard-core terrorist who had an underground armoury. He died there, of a 'heart attack', and among the things to be returned to the bereaved were two large boots with socks that did not match colour.

Now the shoemaker stood facing two homeguards. The homeguards were being motivated by the cry of Arrest, arrest! and no doubt wished they were back in bed. With one of them the small toe of the right foot could be seen quivering in and out of the dirty half-boot while the wide socks which had long lost elasticity lay crumbled inside the boot around the ankle. Arrest, arrest!

"He ought to be shot by a cowboy."

I turned round. The scholar was tightening the belt of his shorts. He stood next to my sister Wangeci, whom he had addressed. But she was either unimpressed by Mwangi's remark or was too angry with me.

"Have you stopped drawing your neat Tarzans on the wall of the teachers' lavatory?" she asked the cowboy. Then catching sight of me she snapped, "You lout! where have you been? What time is it? Where are your shorts?"

I had no time to explain as I handed her the soap. The headman and the full-blooded young reverend had come up and were now greeting my father's daughter with enthusiasm.

She turned away; Jimmy barked; the cowboy hitched his holsters.

Of course they arrested him. I didn't stay there much longer for the teacher had dared me to wait for what would follow if she got home before I did. ("Beautiful face with a beautiful soul to match — like your mother," I said and walked away). But the story had it from the scholar that when they took the shoemaker to the homeguard post he looked at the headman's big boots and, by signs, said he could mend them into a less illogical shape. The scholar had been admitted into the interrogation room by virtue of the fact that he was the reverend's brother and therefore stood to lose part of their plot Number 10 to a rude trespasser. But the shoemaker had remained remarkably calm when, on taking a little more trouble to find out, the headman had realised that the man was not after all being funny (and refusing 'to tell all') but was in fact dumb. Up to now he had only said, Arrest, arrest! for those were the days when no one could be patient with people who refused to 'tell all'. In fact it paid to raise the baton and strike first for otherwise the law-breaker would bandy words with you and waste the government's time. But at the homeguard post the headman (he had reserved for himself the privilege of using the whip, having once worked on a white settler's farm as a labourer, then on the receiving end) fired questions at the shoemaker. All he got was a stutter of loose whining sounds and much gesticulating of the right hand which the stranger swung up and down as if he still held the hammer — or so said the scholar.

"When I saw this, the book fell out of my hands — just like your toilet soap."

But the maturing scholar, who was being groomed in the best institutions of the pictorial paperback and Tarzan and loudly predicted TV in ten years, seemed to close his eyes and caught himself remarkably in the midst of it all. To the young hero, the stranger was an object of unsatisfied dreams through whom he would settle his accounts and shoot the villain off the horse with an accurate shot. It was dangerous because he was young (though I must admit I did in a sense envy him then his knowledge of distant lands). He would no doubt grow up with the impeccable image of white in his mind while he felt deficient that in fact he would remain a black, second rate cowboy. My folk tales embarrassed him, and in effect came to embarrass me too for in due course he convinced me that his great-grandfather and mine had proved themselves quite incapable of inventing gun-powder. And as he recounted his adult brother's complaint that evil villains seemed to have no respect for property these days, one felt that the young preacher nursed a furtive passion for romance himself or he would not have allowed the cowboy to read this kind of stuff. So that when the headman announced that the shoemaker was to be pushed out of the village by the thumb in the manner of his own gesticulations the preacher and the cowboy must have put their smoking guns on the table and washed their folded hands at the breast in triumph.

* * *

Ejected so informally, the shoemaker had vanished as suddenly as he had appeared. Listening to Mwangi, I seemed to see the old man fold his torn tent, throw his unidentified shoes in the sack and the toolbox after them, making his hurried exit up the government's lone road into oblivion. I seemed to see his bent back, his browned rags as they ordered him out in the late afternoon. I could see the sunset on his face; boasting no credentials and wanting none, suspected by all. Jimmy barked at the scholar and I could not but feel too that perhaps I had in a strange way helped to throw the shoemaker out.

But he came back. Just happened. This time it was the friend of D.O. Robinson in person who fell upon him. He had apparently — the whole thing is not clear — taken another liberty to camp where he jolly well liked. And camp he did. Whether it was coincidence, good timing or just sheer defiant design, I cannot tell. But the plot of land where he was now caught actually erecting his tent belonged to a retired money lender, Ngugi, who had been shot two days earlier. He had no children and his wife had deserted him to marry somebody else as he was too thrifty with the cents. Thus his plot seemed to have no immediate claimant. This was unusual because normally one left the sons of the clan — hitherto mostly unheard of — sharpening their weapons while the daughters poisoned one another. But it was as if his very wealth, if he had any, had become taboo. All one saw in fact was a hut that was slowly leaning downhill in the direction of the valley whereas we all expected that he would build the best wooden house to scorn us. He was strange and it seemed fitting in a weird way that his inheritor, for the moment at any rate, should be the strange shoemaker himself. He was now camping without the slightest concern as to the reputation of his benefactor. The headman was in fact coming to burn the hut down for we villagers were quite capable of turning it into an oath-taking house. But on seeing the shoemaker he stopped behind his guards and pushed them forward. More guards could be heard shooting, no doubt tearing and eating sugar cane, down the valley.

I shall not claim first hand information here for the scholar and I were venturing a walk on the deserted outskirts of the village in our best Sunday shorts at that hour. On this occasion he had now let the cowboys be, and he put one hand in his pocket while the other held a cigarette, most likely stolen from his brother's shop. Having witnessed most of his cowboys slay the villain and reach their climax in the heroine's bedroom, Mwangi was now busy astounding me with a lecture on the virtues of sex. Perhaps this was one way of explaining the adult world. (From then on my sister Wangeci did not need to insist I wear shorts.) The sound of shooting down the valley had become our daily bread and one did not stop to think and feel afraid. Somebody always kept us on the move. Somehow you didn't get hit and somehow that strengthened the funny feeling that the worst that was happening to your friends would not happen to you. And yet news of death would come now and then, of a relative or someone one knew.

Even as we stood there experimenting in bawdy talk, I was certain that Munyua had the same feeling that I had; that one was always a little surprised to get home and find that one's immediate guardian or family was intact. We had learnt at our age to be, and yet not to be, concerned too much about life, as we found dead bodies on the path or found a man's blood on our desks at school. We talked and laughed and tried not to distrust, reassuring ourselves that it was indeed possible to be friends despite what our parents warned.

But as we strolled about lazily, I felt this was perhaps why Munyua always read the cowboys. He could not remember his parents who were dead and he could himself once have passed unidentified and detached like the stranger.

He had no blood relation in the location except his brother who patronised him in every sense and made known the fact of his generosity. In effect he had retreated into his own world which assessed any situation on two uncompromising lines like a railway engine, there being, for him, only good and bad cowboys. His guardian's approach to men did not help. For the reverend also focused on a dual pattern of uncompromising debits and credits, all exorbitant actions being allowed for by his old saying that 'One cannot be precise about the soul' and 'When in doubt dismiss as evil'.

And one felt that he had been in doubt about the stranger. If he had not camped on his plot perhaps the reverend would have felt uneasy about anyone discovering a manhandled stranger was in fact dumb only after summoning the law. But this was clearly a matter of Profit and Loss. For how could one be certain that the trespasser would not turn pedlar, selling all kinds of articles and deflecting customers? Wasn't his very camping an assault on the rights of the village preacher, who was esteemed by the headman who in turn spoke well of him to his friend Dorobinson? Inscrutable and aloof, Dorobinson had all the credits on his side. These were passed on to the headman as signified by chevrons which increased more and more down the sleeve according to chickens presented. To anyone else but the preacher, it would have looked like an act of conspiracy, perhaps a compromise of human weaknesses as inherent in the black and the white. Indeed I could envisage the headman as he presented the eggs — if in fact the whole thing was true, there being always cause to doubt organised village gossip. He would stand there wondering if he might not be snubbed after all and if the eggs would be broken with a kick of the boot. But the D.O. would condescend, give him a conspiratorial smile as if to acknowledge the possibility of an occasional fall to the level of the native. Then he would take the eggs and recollect his dignity. It wasn't friendship; they were strangers behind the facade and the danger was that the eggs might become a ceremonial right. But it worked, that was what mattered. There was no immediate worry in the mind of Dorobinson's friend and the conspiracy of hearts and eggs persisted.

Mwangi the cowboy finished his cigarette and we strolled back into the village. Suddenly, Jimmy was running towards us barking, out of nowhere. He licked my rubber shoes. It was curious how he had come to identify himself with me since that eventful morning when the shoemaker appeared. Like him, he was unclaimed as far as I could tell, having found his way into the village — from nowhere. He had dodged the homeguards on several occasions. My beautiful sister Wangeci never accepted him because he would be identified with our plot No. 30. He might bite D. O. Robinson and then we would be called upon to pay for the bullets wasted on a dog rather than a man. I fought to keep him. (I had recently strangled a pup rather than see it shot and its whining as I tightened the rope round its neck was something I never quite recovered from.)

Mwangi stroked Jimmy.

"He seems impatient," he said.

Indeed he was impatient and he would not be led our way. The cowboy and I more or less followed, hilariously cutting across other people's plots, laughing, laughing... The laughter died on our faces.

There on the deceased money lender's plot was the unmistakable tent. The headman stood almost amused, the whip ready. There was a big crowd and he felt the whole situation was under control. Most people had nothing much to do on a Sunday afternoon. It wasn't like the old days when so and so would brew beer and the men of the location found their way there without the formalities of an invitation. Now it was understood that when two or three were gathered together they conspired against the government. Man walked alone. But in this case the headman was present with his homeguards; so it was lawful. I could just make out the shoemaker, his deliberate metallic clang dying on the last with audacious indifference. The reverend flanked the headman as his spiritual complementary and I now watched the show with enthusiasm. But the reverend, who had recently been refused by my sister Wangeci, did not look very concerned. This was not his plot now and he seemed convinced as we all were that the shoemaker's business was unmistakably one of shoes.

Presently a jeep tore its way towards us and we scattered as D. O. Robinson arrived, brandishing two revolvers. It was not often that one saw Dorobinson in person and I had not in fact seen this invisible force behind the headman before. We crowded round once more, this time leaving room among ourselves in case it was necessary to flee. He looked very angry, his face burnt red. The headman greeted his friend.

The D. O. stood facing him. Then he slapped him hard — on both cheeks — and kicked him.

"I understand you steal eggs and kill chickens in my name," he said. He was speaking in a high voice and it was only my sister who seemed to understand all he was saying, although the scholar made desperate attempt. Then the D.O. kicked him some more and told him to get into the jeep.

Wondering what the whole village was doing here anyway, he noticed the shoemaker who was looking at his boots.

"Stranger?" he asked.

No one answered. He made towards him. We held our breath.

"Hey, you!" a voice rang out. "Go and get me a packet of Omo. It washes *brighter* than white!"

It was my beautiful, brave sister Wangeci, and she was addressing me. But it had the desired effect. The D.O. turned upon Wangeci. She held her ground as he stared at her. The reverend fell in behind him, looking at Wangeci more like a goat on heat than a faithful servant of the law. The shoemaker hammered on; Jimmy barked and the D.O. left.

He stayed. And he saved our soles. Looking back on the whole affair now, one feels he was a mystery. He remained inscrutable behind that forehead which thrust itself forward while the eyes shrunk in and stared, blankly. He would not 'tell all'. I wonder if he was not slightly insane too. For a man who could endure so much knocking about might as well build himself a world where the distractions of the imagination would at least smooth the harness. And as I pass by his small shop which years later has fallen into the less remarkable hands of a grocer, I wonder if we could be condemned for distrusting him at first. It soon became evident, however, that his one purpose in life was to mend our sickly soles which seemed to approach the roads of life from all kinds of illogical directions.

Soon everyone brought their shoes to him. This included the new headman, who never paid, and the reverend who sent them shyly through the cowboy. Less competent shoemakers who were scattered here and there conspired to start their own partnerships in competition, broke up because they could not trust one another, and gave up the whole leather business to try something else. A man like that had many debtors for he never seemed in a hurry to get paid. Naturally we exploited him. But as soon as business seemed to flourish, he pulled down the tent and erected a wooden hut which looked more like a kennel than a man's house. And in a village where everyone endeavoured to be one up on everyone else (although one did not want to appear too rich for fear of thieves and terrorists) he remained remarkably unconcerned as to our opinion of him.

We became frequent visitors to his hut, the cowboy, Jimmy and I. Having erected the wooden hut he did not seek an official acknowledgement of our acceptance of him by getting the Government sign-writer to paint a neat number on the door. He did it himself. He bought some red paint. Then with a piece of beaten leather, he put the sign of the cross on the door and smiled at us. Mwangi was immediately appalled and ran for his brother. But since the shoemaker did not seem to start another religion (he only remained remarkably detached) the reverend cowered and minded his shop.

He frequently got into trouble. Once the terrorists came, apologised for having to collect all the boots, and escaped into the forest. Another lot, who did not apologise, came and beat him, stealing all the nails, for some purpose or other. And I remember a white soldier once ordering him to polish his boots. The shoemaker looked at the neat boots which had a little dust, at the thick socks which matched colour — a sign of 'good' organisation — and declined the privilege. Again he was beaten up. But he seemed to forget it all and the deliberate, uninterrupted hammering could be heard tearing steadily away the next morning.

* * *

He disappeared. Disappeared as suddenly as he had come. It all seemed like a silly joke but this time he never came back. I still remember it was twilight as I came home from school late and I suddenly caught sight of a figure disappearing over the horizon, with a dog trotting by its side. I did not need to be told. The two beings had become inseparable friends, the one making unnatural, detached sounds which Jimmy acknowledged by occasional barks.

I went to the hut to confirm if indeed he had gone. I only saw a number of shoes, all mended and left there for the owners to collect.

* * *

That was fifteen years ago and now we have moved out of the village for it is no longer necessary to be taken care of. (Many things have happened since. Wangeci eventually ran off with the preacher. He was advised by his superiors to choose between preaching and business and preferred the latter. "The old goat!" my father shouted at Wangeci one evening. "Says he won't pay the dowry because he is better than a pagan, did he? I swear by your mother's kindly soul your brother and I will castrate him yet..." But the old goat didn't cough a cent and we didn't castrate him.) And as I recall those times the thing that looms largest in a hazy memory is the peculiar stranger. I can see him nursing the shoe carefully in the hand as clearly as I did then. I can see us barefooted children and cowboys — whom he loved and tolerated — standing by the number-less door or sitting in the sun, watching him condemn another old shoe to a new sole. Now and then he takes the shoe in his hand, holds it a few inches from his face (it seems *now* that he was short-sighted) and regards it with a keen sense of detail. Perhaps it is a heavy boot or a light shoe, black, brown or a lady's white but the story will be the same. There is something the matter with it and what is wrong is that it needs mending.

That seems to be the simple logic.

Perhaps he will take a sympathetic look at the customer as if to read his ways from the heel. And the uneasy customer who thinks this impertinent may ask, When? knowing very well that he should expect nothing more articulate than a grunt which seems to say, Badly worn, badly worn... And you stand fascinated as the shoemaker turns the shoe meticulously in his hand, like a surgeon ready with his scalpel. When? How much? the customer asks again. Whereupon the shoemaker takes another pitying look at him and tosses the shoe over the shoulder into a pile of unmended ones. He continues to work on the shoe that was in his hand before the customer entered. After a stitch here and a stitch there, he retrieves the shoe from the pile and gives it a bang on the heel. If he bangs once that will mean, Come and collect it tomorrow; if twice, the next day and so on. (He never mentions money.) Then we all watch the client jog his way out in varied contortions that seem to strike the shoemaker as exceedingly frightful for he is shaking his head. Jimmy, who has now found a permanent mate, barks after the disappearing form too, as if to warn him to take the path more reasonably.

Then the scholar takes his book and reads on, while I go to buy some toilet soap, same as always, to keep our own legs clean.

five

esther

Excitement was rife in the atmosphere. It was in the weird music of the wind as it swept across the valley caressing the trees on the hillside. The myriad fingers of the thicket, black in the twilight, danced savagely to the wild beat of the frogs downstream. Boy and dog jumped across the stream startling the insects in the lush grass on the bank. The little caverns of the thicket bristled with life. To their ears came the squelch and the rustle that the object of their chase made in its struggles to reach safety in the heart of the thicket. The squelching ceased. The rustling receded and died in the mild commotion.

"We've lost him," said the boy and sighed deeply. "And gosh! It's late!"

The dog edged nearer and the boy felt the warm body rubbing against his bare leg. The sun had long crept behind the western wall of mountains, and the sky was a darkening mauve. A jackal cried out in blasphemy and the reverberated sound was an eerie moan in the valley. The boy shivered.

"Let's go back," he said, remembering the danger that lurked all round, in the woods and in the bushes. As they teemed with prey so did these woods seethe with the new danger. Perhaps in the house every heart was already beating for him, every lip breathing a silent prayer.

The sweat of remorse broke on his brow and confusedly he crossed the stream again.

"Come on, Ciri!" he urged impatiently. Reluctantly, the dog turned and gracefully leapt to his side. He caressed him with a hand, a second weight tugging on his heart. He had shattered the dog's awakened hopes and crushed his spirits. How could he make him see that for his sake he had disobeyed his mother, risking her wrath to allow him a breath of the sweet, rare air of freedom in the exciting wild? Too late the hunt had started, most of the wild fowl having gone back to their nests to await tomorrow and too soon it had stopped. With nothing to boast of they would go back home.

He remembered Ciri's look half an hour before. The dog had come up to him after he had arrived home from school and had looked at him with sad, pleading eyes that had made his heart bleed. For the past week he had been lying around the house, a perfect picture of boredom and misery. With his eyes he had pleaded for a change — for mercy. The boy's mother had not returned from communal duty at the post. His father had had an accident there the day before and was lying in bed. A short run into the woods would probably not be noticed. His mother perhaps would never find out. And Ciri needed it.

He had led him to the gate. They had stood there outside listening to Nature's quiet murmur. The leaves had fluttered in the fields. And Nature had beckoned. Their hearts rippling with excitement they had run down the garden path beyond the boundary of their garden into the rich, tangled mass of vegetation on the hillside. Every bush had been tempting and irresistible. Time had slipped away unheeded. 'The danger' if indeed it moved in the woods went quietly about its business.

The heated chase of their only prey in that hour, a rabbit, had brought them thundering and panting to the stream where the sudden challenge of the forbidding thicket growing on its bank had awakened them to the consciousness of time.

As he chained the dog for the night his heart was heavy and he wondered what his mother would say. She had most solemnly warned him against wandering around after school. He was to come straight home and confine himself to the house.

"The terrorists don't know who is for them or who is against," she had said. "Sometimes they'll hide in the bush waiting for the darkness to come. What will happen when you run into them?"

With equal solemnity of face he had dramatically run his hand across his throat.

She had laughed. "They don't know who is good and who is bad," she had said.

Neither did he. Everyone seemed to hate and fear both the homeguards and the terrorists they protected them from. Once he and his mother had watched stricken with horror as two homeguards beat up his father with gun-butts. Yet his father always prayed that the terrorists would be overcome. His mother called the homeguards devils. Few of them, she always said, had the guts to face their real enemies. So they beat up innocent people.

"The terrorists are even more cowardly," his father had once replied. "Who are they fighting, I want to know? The villages they have burnt! The innocent lives they have taken! Everywhere they go they kill their own because they can't get at the white people. And those are the thieves of the land," he had added in lowered tones.

"The black people who have refused to take oaths are not their own," his mother had replied quietly. "They are Europeans at heart. That is why they kill them."

"They kill innocent children too," his father had flashed back indignantly.

"Yes," his mother had replied calmly, "The larvae of the weevil must go with the parent."

It seemed strange to him that after the whites had stolen the land the blacks should divide and wage a bitter war among themselves to regain the land none of them had stolen. For such to his young mind seemed to be the state of the matter.

Afraid to face his parents after his escapade, he wanted to go into his grandmother's hut. Then he remembered she had moved in with the rest of the family the day before. Always at loggerheads with her daughter-in-law she had been most reluctant to take this move although his father had constantly urged her to. Finally, after the murder of the chief by an unidentified gang, the fire of panic ate across the entire country and her protests were stilled. She had left the hut.

He stood at the door trying to make up a story. But he knew it was no use. The absence of Ciri must have been noted and the truth known — or guessed at.

He shrugged in resignation and knocked on the door.

"Who is it?" The tremulous voice of his grandmother sounded tense and anxious from within.

He said it was only him, and his sister Njeri recognised his voice and opened the door. The house was smoky and dimly lit and the mixed smells of smoke and food cooking on the fire was unpleasant after the fresh night air.

"Mburu!" cried his grandmother, "Where have you been?"

He entered the room and closed the door. The absence of his mother was a relief to him. Before he could reply, she said,

"I thought you were together with your mother. Where is she?"

"I don't know," he said, "I have not seen her."

"Where can she be?" She looked very worried.

He took one of his books and began to read by the light of the smoky kerosene lamp. His worry was over.

Sometime afterwards his grandmother's voice interrupted him.

"Where can she be . . . . ?"

Startled he looked up. Both his grandmother and sister wore very worried faces. Suddenly he felt chilled at heart too. On other nights when she went out his mother told them and never stayed out very long.

"Should we wake up father?" asked Nyeri helplessly.

"No," her grandmother replied hoarsely. "What can he do? Let him rest."

"How is his leg?" Mburu asked.

She shook her head as if to say it was worse.

"It is inflamed," she said, "Earlier on we squeezed out the pus and washed the wound with salt. He felt better. Let him rest."

"Oh, this post!" Mburu said. "I wish it would be finished soon."

"After they have dug the trench it will be," she said, "But that will not be the end of the work. I have heard that they will clear the bush next. The Government wants it cleared."

"The bush!" he exclaimed.

"Yes," his grandmother replied, "The wood too might be cleared. Then the terrorists can't hide there."

That would be the end of everything, he thought. He always hoped that after the danger was all over he and Ciri would resume their interrupted adventure trips in the wood. If it were cleared there would be no more joy in life. This epoch of darkness would extend over eternity.

When supper was served it was tasteless in his mouth. Everyone looked at the dying coals of the neglected fire as if they could provide the answer to the question in their hearts. Nobody talked much.

But when the bowls were carefully stacked away after the meal a feeling of lightness spread over him. He found little cause to worry over his mother. This was not the first time she was out at night. She often went out to see a neighbour. When his father raised protests saying it was dangerous she laughed at him. She was so strong and full of courage and fire. If she came in and found them sitting miserably round the fire, worrying over her, she would just burst out laughing.

"She often goes out to Njoroge's home to see his wife Nduta," he said, thinking it wise to let his grandmother know it really was not all that strange for his mother to be out at night.

"At night?" she asked incredulously.

"At night," he said.

"The fool! It is dangerous," she said. "Somehow I feel that something is wrong."

Mburu looked at his grandmother and felt sorry for her. Already she looked older. The lines of her face, probably due to some trick of the light, looked deeper and more intricate.

"Perhaps the terrorists — but God will help her!" said the poor soul.

"Suppose they have!" Njeri gasped in alarm.

"No — but we cannot be sure. Mburu!"

The boy looked up.

"There is no sense in waiting any longer. Listen!"

Some moments later he tiptoed to the back of the house. Ciri rose in surprise and approached him in the darkness. As he bent down to unbuckle the heavy chain he felt the dog's hot breath on his cheek and smelt his warm body.

"Come on, Ciri," he said in an urgent whisper.

The dog grunted in pleasure and followed his master quietly in the darkness. They came up to the road and broke into a trot. Then Mburu realised that it might be dangerous: their footfalls were too loud as they ran.

The trip was a tense one but fortunately short. He breathed a sigh of relief as he came to the path that led down the hillside to Njoroge's home. "Ask them if they know anything about your mother," his grandmother had instructed. As the house came in sight — a large silhouette in the darkness — fear settled on his heart. He could feel that she was not there, that indeed some misfortune had befallen her.

The gate, when he came to it, was locked from the inside. He paused for a moment and then clambered over it. It squeaked and groaned on its rusty hinges and the sound was terrifying in the silent night. When he jumped over to the other side and got up to his feet the dog stood waiting on the dewy grass. From the edges of a wooden window light filtered through.

They walked together past the cow-shed and the barn and their feet froze. The cool air was delicately tainted with a putrid smell from the cow-shed.

He knocked on the door gently. The next moment the house was in darkness. Not a whisper came from within. He stood surprised for a moment. The feeling of danger became very real to him. The reaction of those inside made him feel suddenly naked and unprotected from the evil they thought was now upon them.

With a shiver he turned and retraced his steps to the gate. Quite obviously his mother was not here. The one thought in his mind now was get back home to the warm fireside. Fear had mounted in his heart.

Even as he got back to the road he hesitated. Back at home his grandmother and sister were waiting fearfully .... Waiting for the news he would bring them. Here he was going back with nothing to report. He had not even talked to Njoroge. His brave trip in the darkness had achieved nothing. Rather than alleviate the fear in their hearts his fruitless return would crush their hopes. The prospect was repelling. As he hesitated on the road an idea budded in his mind and grew and soon he was engrossed in it.

In the distance the post was a tall silhouette. Earlier on in the week he had passed near the post and the guard on the watch tower had called his name. His surprise had known no bounds. He had looked up and recognised the grinning face of an old friend. His name was Ndungu and the last time he had seen him he had been a labourer. Mburu had not heard of his joining the homeguards.

If anybody could help it was Ndungu. During the day when the people had been working at the post Ndungu must have seen his mother. If she had been locked inside the post by the guards as he had heard people quite often were, Ndungu would know. At any rate he would go home with the feeling that he had tried.

"Come on, Ciri," his voice was quiet and firm.

They hastened towards the post. Ciri ran by his side certainly bewildered by all this clandestine wandering yet delighted at being once more active beside his master.

They drew near and the post loomed large before them. They derived no comfort from the thought that within the post were the guardians of the peace. People wandering around at night were always suspected of being in league with terrorists.

But Ndungu knew him...

A few yards from the great doors of the post he stopped. He could see nothing. He could hear nothing either save the anxious beating of his heart and Ciri's breathing. He looked up the dark watch tower. Should he call? He was too scared to try.

Suddenly the watch-tower opened a large dazzling eye and he gasped with the suddenness of it. He shaded his eye from the torch beam. Ciri let out a bark.

"Who goes there?" a voice shouted from high up. The torch beam was searching his face, the dog's body — and all around. "Name yourself!"

His voice trembled as he said faintly, "Mburu . . ."

The guard had certainly not heard but he asked, "Is there anybody else with you?" The beam of light circled all around him.

"No," Mburu said shaking his head.

"Tell that dog to shut up."

He patted Ciri on the head and quietened him in a choked voice.

"Open the gate," the homeguard said to someone within.

Mburu heard some voices inside and the next minute the gates opened with groans of protest. At the same time another torch beam glared in his face. The beam lighted his way up to the gate and a man warned him to be careful where he stepped. He walked over the draw-bridge to the gateway where two guards, stolid and grim-looking in their heavy coats, waited.

He stammered out his story while the man listened silently. He could not see their faces but he could tell from their voices that Ndungu was not among them.

The gates were closed and locked once more and he was led through a corridor.

"Your grandmother is an old idiot," said the guard in front of him. "She must have been mad to send you into the night like that. Murdering terrorists are loose all over the country. What a woman!"

He gathered courage. "Mother —" he stammered, "Is she here?"

"No," the guard said. "What is her name?"

"Esther."

"Esther!" Said the guard behind him. "I think I know her. She's a mad one."

His heart sank and misery flooded his heart. He waited to go back but he knew they would not hear of it. His grandmother and sister, not knowing his fate, would not be able to sleep that night. But above all he worried over his mother whom he had so utterly failed to find.

* * *

As she came up the path that led to the house the wind rustled her dress and she pulled her overcoat closer about her. There was a tight, tense feeling in her breast and she was breathing hard. She was exhausted after the run. She looked to the east and shook off a growing feeling of nausea.

There was a little line of light under the door. She smiled a little. How worried everyone must be. They were such jumpy creatures. She gave the door a knock and there was a quick sound. The door was flung open and she stood framed in the doorway. Njeri gasped with relief and flung her arms around her, digging her face into her breast.

"Mother...." She cried overcome with emotion, "Oh, mother."

Esther pushed her away gently.

"Come on now," she said in bewilderment. "Don't cry. And I warned you never to open the door without making sure that it is a friend's knock."

"Oh, but I knew it was you," said the girl as she closed the door again, "I knew it would be either you or Mburu. It had to be."

"Always make sure," Esther said firmly. She was glad to be back. Away from everything — leaving the men to it all. But for some time the tense feeling in her breast would continue .... She warmed her hands over the fire and suddenly a frown came to her face.

"Mburu? Where is he?"

She looked from her daughter to her mother-in-law. The old woman stared back across the smoky fire.

"Where have you been, Esther?" She asked evasively.

"Just around," shrugged Esther, "What is it? You all look — but where is Mburu?"

There was silence. Her mother-in-law looked afraid to meet her eyes. Then she said in a tired voice.

"He is out looking for you, Esther. He is gone to Njoroge's home."

Esther stiffened. Her lips twitched a little.

"Looking.... for me?" She breathed.

"Yes, Esther," The voice of the old woman rose in anxiety. "We were all worried to death about you. It was late. The darkness was thick. I —"

"You sent him to look for me?" Esther's voice was hoarse.

"I sent him to Njoroge's home," her mother-in-law said feebly. Desperately she added, "I was distressed."

Esther was breathing hard. She turned to her daughter. "Is that so?" she asked but the girl was mute and downcast. Then she turned upon the old woman and this time fire was in her eyes.

"You stupid crab ... Stupid old crab ... Suppose he is killed? Suppose my son is killed! Tonight — why tonight!"

"He is all right, Mother," Njeri interposed suddenly, "He wasn't going far."

Esther paid no heed. "Oh, Mother, Mother Maria. Why tonight?"

Suddenly she turned and made for the door.

"Where are you going?" The old woman asked in alarm.

"I am going for him!"

"No!" she said.

Esther turned. A bitter look came to her face.

"What is a mother supposed to do?" she asked. Her voice shook.

The next moment she had gone back into the night. Njeri called out her name and followed. But her mother had disappeared down the path. Njeri stood there calling her in the darkness and suddenly she burst into tears. Then she was chilled by a sound that rang out in the still night and rumbled in the distance. Her grandmother had heard it too and she came quickly out of the house.

"I don't think it's mother," Njeri whispered to reassure her. "It came from the post." Their eyes were turned eastwards to the direction the shot had come from. Then they caught their breath as the night suddenly seemed to explode with a bright yellow light and the post began to blaze.

six

the village pastor

Reverend Johnson K. Mwaura was known to be a good man. Above all, he was known to be as good a Christian as they come. Perhaps that's not saying very much for they did come well below the mark in our village. But it is enough to say that he had run his own life enviably, and had at least endeavoured to navigate his household as close to the scriptural waters as possible.

Well, of course, there was his son Kamau who ministered the oath in the forest, but that could have happened to any father.

No one in the village had anything against the pastor, for he never intended any man a bad turn. Soft spoken except when in combat with Satan at the pulpit, he had a kind of bedside manner towards the sickly souls of the Lord's flock which perhaps might have hurt the more sensitive. But any such apparently patronising attitude was not meant. It only arose from the fact that he saw it as his personal responsibility, with God's mercy, to mete out the cup to these trodden souls.

Looking at that unflinching, unmoveable horde of sinners, one would have felt sorry for the ageing reverend. For his Sabbath audience — especially the menfolk — consisted of sinners half-asleep, sinners half-drunk, sinners who still wore Saturday night shirts, sinners still smelling of Saturday night indulgences. Some of them did not much care whether their hangover sobered down at home or in the serenity of the Lord's house and were successfully dragged off to church by their wives. A few were intercepted and diverted to church on their way to Muriuki's.

Everyone knew Muriuki's. You had only to ask your way there and you were a stranger. Wives who had for months to pull their husbands from Muriuki's or kids who went to Muriuki's and got duly kicked out for reminding their fathers that the headmaster was still after the school fees, had long been acquainted with the spot in their own ways.

Not that it would have worried the padre very much. He had resigned himself to the salvation of the more tender souls that didn't frequent bars yet still remained kind of blemished in this world of sins. But as it was, the bar was virtually next door to his church. As he left his house, Bible in hand, riding to church on his bicycle, sinners watched him through their windows. Others he passed promised they would be with him in the Lord's house as soon as their feet got them there.

"We have not the pleasure of riding there, pastor," they said.

But "there" turned out to be Muriuki's where most men of the village sought escapism.

Now on this wet Christmas day, Reverend J. K. Mwaura was particularly perturbed. Particularly disturbed because the Lord's birthday fell on a Sunday. Pockets were full with the Christmas bonus. As he stood at the pulpit and addressed the faithful sheep who had answered the call to sing the carols good and loud, the Reverend solemnly said,

"Brethren, we are gathered yet again in humble submittance of our souls to the keeping of Him who guideth and protecteth us, this morning under His roof ...."

Rain trickled through the roof. Drops of rain had for some years now dug holes on the bare floor of the church and where such holes happened to be, the audience kept away.

"...... Two years ago today brethren, you will recall the full house that the Lord was pleased to have sing and praise Him. Since then sisters, er, sisters *and* brothers, you have beheld the work of the devil. Satan has built a rival house next door. And the sinners house has lured them all.

"It is the same road to that sinners' abode as it is to here. But I tell you, sisters, it is a wide road and they will not know how wide until the day of judgement!

"I ask you, brethren, is it righteous that the Lord should abide under a rusty roof while the devil takes premises under sparkling corrugated iron? Two years ago, I appealed for generous donations so that we can honour God with a much more reverent church. What do we witness instead? Must we, by declining to tax ourselves generously, tax the patience of Jehovah? Remember Sodom and Gomorrah!"

You could have heard a pin fall on the Lord's earthen floor.

"Brethen, I ask you, where are all these people?" *(all these people* being the supposed occupants of the empty benches). "Last night, sisters, er, sisters and brothers, I assembled my household together so we could pray for a full house today. It was then that I found that my second son had been missing since morning. On pursuing the issue, I was informed that he was under that roof! My own son!"

Furious with anger, the pastor decided to take a firmer line and tow the devil out of the deep sea where he lay inebriated, on to the shore of reason.

"Brethren!" he shouted, "arise, follow me, for today we're going to take the Word right into that house!"

A less determined man would have been put off by the sacrilegious singing that was to be heard coming from Muriuki's. But not the pastor. He marched vigorously in at a pace that could have been suitably accompanied with "When the Saints Go Marching In." He stood at the counter, open bible in both hands. The larger part of his own audience remained outside as Muriuki's was crammed to near capacity in the spirit of the Christmas season. Some wives, however, did manage to join their husbands to persuade them to listen to 'the wise word of the pastor.'

The dramatic entry of the reverend had caused silence in the bar. It was too early yet for most of the men to be effectively drunk. Besides the pastor was held in high esteem. He encountered no angry outburst.

"Brothers", he began, "you will find the Lord's own version of the song you were blaspheming just now in hymn number ——. As no doubt you do not have your hymn books with you, my own audience will be pleased to join and lead you at your tables.

Jesus is tenderly calling thee home —
Calling to-day, calling to-day!
Why from the sunshine of love wilt thou roam,
Farther and farther away?
Call—..ing today! Call—..ing today!
Je—..sus is call—..ing today!

None of the men sang even that first verse. By now they had sufficiently recovered from their surprise to say,

"What's the idea, pastor?" It was Muriuki, the bar owner. Reverend J. K. Mwaura had not seen him for months. It hurt him, and the Lord, to see the man who was responsible for all this. He rarely lost his temper. But now, seeing himself so impiously interrupted he snapped,

"Get thee behind the Lord, Satan!" It was the language the devil would understand best. But he did not carry on in this vein. He skilfully won attention without a murmur of any more protest. He spoke at length on evils lately manifest in the life of the village since 'the devil took residence'.

School fees that remained unpaid, wives who now hardly got a cent to run their homes, kids who went in tattered shirts . . .

He was soon reduced to tears and the women were moved. But not the men. They took their mugs.

"Why didn't you at least build your bar far from my church?" he asked, turning to Muriuki.

"It was the only plot of land I had. That's why some are fighting in the forest, pastor."

This brought murmurs of approval. Everybody understood. But the pastor held his ground.

"Mau Mau can't fight the white man for land by dividing the souls of their own kind."

"We are divided already, pastor," Muriuki said promptly. "The white man has lured some people to fight us as home guards."

"And you?"

Muriuki smelt this as dangerous ground. Few in that bar knew that he spied on the white man and his followers for the Mau Mau terrorists.

"Me, pastor?" he said, "I am a peaceful citizen. All I ask is, leave me alone. I do not force anyone to drink in my bar. You might try my beer. It's good." There was an outburst of laughter. The pastor didn't think it funny.

"Reverend, we know you for a good man but what do you want with some of us?"

He looked round. It was Kairu who had spoken.

"Just look at me, reverend," he said pointing to his right leg, amputated at the knee. "You think I would worship God any more? This is no black man who has done this to me."

"Jesus," said the reverend, "wasn't an Englishman. He was a Jew, and not even a Jew but God for us all."

"Well, what's the difference? A white man is a white man anywhere," Kairu insisted, looking round for approval. He got it.

For fifteen minutes, the reverend went on preaching on the theme of brotherhood and love that knew no colour. Every man, black or white, must keep their lamps ready or theirs would be a plight worse than that of the five foolish virgins. And when the doors closed, some, the cleansed, would be welcomed within but those to be found wanting even because of an iota of sin would be locked without to gnash teeth forever in the fire of gehenna.

At last, exhausted, he took out his handkerchief, wiped his brows, and asked those who would to follow him so as to conclude the sermon in God's own House. He was surprised to see his audience only a little bigger than before when at last he settled at the pulpit. One or two more had come from the village for the excitement.

"Brothers and sisters," the reverend said, "look at the marvels of the Lord. One extra bench! Let us pray —

"Oh, Lord, thou didst say that when two or three —"

Reverend Johnson K. Mwaura looked up. The drunken were at last bringing their sins from the bar to the altar in a rush. Led by a terrorist, they were kneeling down hurriedly with the pious faces of sinners come home to roost.

".. that when two, three, or more are gathered together in thy name —"

"Hands up!"

Outside, a shot rang into the air. Everybody stood up. At the door, a young white soldier stood pointing his bayonetted rifle all over the church. They called them "Johnnies" for that's what the white soldiers called one another.

Johnnie said hands up, and would the preacher tell him where a terrorist who must have taken shelter in the church had rushed to. "Produce him, reverend," he said, "I'll count one minute".

"Young man," Reverend Mwaura fired back in English, "Get o-u-t. This is no place to be soiled by sinners of any colour. Were I to believe that any in the Lord's congregation this morning came here with designs to wreck my service, I would throw them out myself. But when the Word is said, there can be none so blemished whom the Lord will throw out of the warmth of his church, cold and alone. Not even the terrorist you look for. Don't you worship God where you come from that you should storm in like this? Look at your boots!"

Johnnie who must have been newly recruited and about twenty four, looked at the pound of mud on each boot and felt a little ashamed that he should storm in like that.

"Won't you scrape the mud and join us on the day of our Lord?"

"Sorry, reverend, duty calls, duty . . But blast it, man, the bugger must be somewhere!"

"You might try that house there."

"Which one, pastor?" the soldier asked, almost respectfully.

"That bar, yonder!"

"We have been there pastor but there is nobody. It looked deserted."

"Then cast the hunter's eye farther afield," the reverend said rather severely and turned to his bible.

The terrorist may have strayed off to the forest. But he did not consider him one beyond salvation. It was merely a question of welcoming a prodigal who had come home to Christ. In the eyes of the Lord, all those who had just entered were welcome. They had meandered abroad on the devil's wide road. But their sins, when laid at the pulpit, were no less pardonable or blacker than the irreverent butting in of the white youth. Again, he asked the soldier to take off his hat, bring his sins to the altar — never mind the language barrier — and braced himself for the sermon of his life.

But Johnnie felt silly, left, and the pastor, sorry to see a sinner go, continued the prayers amidst whispers of admiration.

". . . . Thou shalt grant their request. We humbly ask thee, therefore, that as we this day recall the coming of thy Son, thou shalt grant us —"

Reverend Johnson K. Mwaura looked up again and this time almost collapsed. Only a few minutes ago he had the largest audience in months. But once again Muriuki's was beating the Lord. These men had fled the bar when word came that the soldiers were again on the hunt. They would have given them a busy day at the home guards' post — but for the refuge of the church. At the sight of the thinning benches, the ageing reverend dropped into tears and the service came to an end.

Two years later Reverend Johnson K. Mwaura died. We buried him behind the church that had been his life on earth. There was a deep silence and no one could doubt the great love and respect that the villagers had for him as a man. Sinners half-drunk, sinners time-off from Muriuki's to pay their last, true-hearted respects, sinners who had now changed yesterday night's dirty shirt for the occasion, were gathered together in a larger audience than the pastor could ever have mustered when he was alive. In rancid but sincere breath they murmured,

"God rest his soul."

Then they departed — quietly back to Muriuki's.

seven

departure at dawn

Mugo came home drenched to the skin. He was panting hard as he kicked the little wooden gate back and hurried along the path, his suffering head bent low, to his hut. He was cursing bitterly — cursing the rain, cursing himself, and even the memsahib.

"Drown me," he hissed under his breath probably to the angry heavens. He added, "Maybe I will be better off dead."

A gust of wind howled across the yard and for a moment he thought it would sweep him away. With it the rain increased, roaring in his ears and blinding him.

He staggered across the bare muddy space of ground. His boots squelched in the mud and in his hurry he almost fell. But now the old hut was only a few yards away; shelter and peace were only a few yards away.

Peace. . . ?

He almost stopped in his tracks. Would there be peace for him anymore? Was he ready to go into the old hut and tell a wounded man — his own brother — that he must go, go sick as he was? And when he went would there be peace...?

He ran the few final yards to the old hut. He pressed his body to the damp crumbling wall thankful for the comparative safety under the eaves of the hut.

Inside the hut were his brother, Ndonga, and his seventeen year old son Karanja. Until he heard their voices Mugo was not aware of his son's presence in the hut. In fact what with all the hurry and the worries of the day he had forgotten that Karanja was due to come home from school that day for the holidays.

Karanja had arrived home two hours before. From the onset his holiday had been overshadowed by a threatening cloud. As usual he had passed through the farm on his way home to have a word with his father. The memsahib's house, large and majestic on the little hill on which it stood had been a refreshing and indeed thrilling sight after three long months of absence.

A path skirted the homestead and ran down the hill to the labourers' camp which squatted in the valley below. Through the fence he could see Peter and Cynthia, two of Memsahib's children riding their tricycles on the lawn. They certainly seemed to have grown! He stood watching them with a smile until he was aware of the weight of the box he carried. Then he had turned and walked down the path to the labourers' camp to look up the headman's family. He would leave his box with the wife and go out into the ranch looking for his father.

The headman's children were playing in the dust when he came up. They ran up to him excitedly and clutched at his clothes and arms soiling him all over. But he was not displeased. It was wonderful coming home again — for the ranch was a second home to Karanja.

It was the headman's wife who told him about his father's dismissal.

Now in the dimness of the hut he sat by his uncle's bedside listening to him talk. It all seemed like a dream — the presence of this strange man who they said was his father's brother. There might have been some likeness between him and his father but with his very long hair and rough beard it was difficult to believe the relationship existed. But when he spoke one was immediately convinced for the voice was the same: quiet, rather husky.

"Don't go to him!" his mother had warned earlier on, "Don't meddle with the man."

"All right," he had replied, "I'll just peep in and have a look at him."

"But do not —"

"I'll just look, Mother. After all, is he not my uncle?"

It had been drizzling when he went out from the new large house towards the old hut. Then suddenly without warning the heavens had opened and the rain had roared in his ears. He had run on into the hut shutting the door behind him hurriedly. Then he was staring at the man on the bed. The man was staring back...

Here he was. A ***real*** terrorist. That hair .... Those eyes... For a moment there was a tight feeling in his breast and his hand felt for the door handle. Then the terrorist grinned.

"*Niu ucio*?" "And who is that?"

Karanja swallowed twice.

"Mugo's eldest son, no doubt. My biggest nephew. You were named after my father, I suppose?"

Karanja nodded, "Yes, I am Karanja."

He had awkwardly gone across to the bed and shaken the hard strong hand the terrorist offered.

That had been almost two hours ago. It was still raining and so he had not gone back yet. He was in no hurry to go back. He watched his uncle roll up some tobacco with a light piece of brown paper. Tough man, this. If all those stories he'd been telling were true.

"How is your leg, now?"

"Terrible," Ndonga replied with a wry smile.

Karanja wondered how his uncle had been shot. In a night raid no doubt. He looked at his uncle thoughtfully. How come a terrorist could be a pleasant fellow? Why, he was quite human. Terrorists burnt, raped and cut off people's heads. Somehow Karanja could not imagine his uncle hacking off people's heads. Some burning, some raping maybe.. But not the other thing.

"When I get back I shall be all right," Ndonga went on, "I shall be treated with herbs. It's just —"

"Who shot you?" Karanja asked, unable to contain his curiosity.

Ndonga turned and for a moment Karanja was frightened. The eyes had slightly narrowed, the nostrils were dilated.

"A white bitch," said the terrorist. "A white bitch. Ngai, she might have killed me!"

Karanja stared at him. He didn't know what to think. He could not understand the look on the man's face. Was it fury? It looked more like fear. He managed a feeble smile.

"You might have killed *her,*" he pointed out. He was glad of the line the conversation was going. Soon, he hoped, his uncle would start talking like a real terrorist. All those stories about hares and bees were all very funny but he had to have something *bloody* for his school mates when he got back to Kikuyu.

"She might have killed me," Ndonga said and this time his face broke into a little amused smile. "But fortunately she only got me in the leg." He shook his head, "That's not the way to die — by a woman's hand."

"Death is always a fearful thing. To me it would make no difference whence it comes," said Karanja. "Whoever kills deserves death too. Don't you think so?"

His uncle smiled, "You are a big fellow. You look sensible too. So I shall talk frankly to you. But no —" he said checking himself, "Your father would not like it."

"I know," said the boy, "But how will he ever know what you told me?"

"Ah, no," said Ndonga seriously, "Your father is risking his life to save me. That is not something a man easily forgets. I would very much like a youth like you to see the truth and the light — what I fight for and why I have lived like a beast in my own country for many years. But your father and your mother would not like it. Their way of thinking is so different from mine."

Karanja did not insist. Instead he changed the subject. "Mother tells me some shocking news. My father has lost his job. When I passed through the farm on my way here the headman's wife told me the same thing. But neither of them know why my father lost his job."

Ndonga chuckled. Why, Karanja had no idea.

"The woman is scared. All the white people are now scared stiff. They trust no black man. I believe she mistrusted your father."

"But that just isn't possible!" Karanja exclaimed. "Father isn't Mau Mau. His family isn't Mau Mau. Nob —" he stopped. His eyes met his uncle's. That was it! Someone knew about his uncle. Whoever that someone was he did not know his uncle's present whereabouts or they would surely have come for him, but they knew that his father had a relative who was a terrorist. The memsahib like many other settlers had informers among her "wogs" and one of them must have told her that his father could not be trusted. In her state of mind (which could easily be imagined after so many settlers had been cut to pieces or shot) the memsahib could not have argued. Strange that she had not had him arrested or shot...

Karanja felt fear creeping all through him. Suddenly the idea of a terrorist in their home ceased to be exciting and became a serious frightening business. The homeguards were always searching houses for hidden guns and ammunition. If they chanced to swoop down upon their house their uncle would surely be found. He would be shot — and so would Karanja's father. The fate of the rest of the family would be something awful too.

"Uncle," he said quietly — and somehow the word did not sound strange. "How is your leg now?"

"Terrible," Ndonga replied and Karanja remembered he had already asked the question before.

"How — soon can you walk?"

His uncle turned and looked at him sombrely.

"I don't know. I can't say," he replied. "A week more, maybe."

"A week! But that is — They will come searching this place and they will find you. And then —"

"They will shoot me." His uncle's voice was cool.

Curse the man. He could only see himself being shot. Besides him he could not see Karanja's poor father. With one bullet they would finish off his innocent father whose only mistake had been having too soft a spot for his murdering brother.

He must go, Karanja decided. If father can't see that I am very surprised... His uncle's voice broke into his line of thought.

"Needless to say," he said, "Your lives are in danger because of me. If they find me here they will be very cruel to you. They might even finish off your father along with me."

"How can we stop this? Uncle, why can't you just cut your hair and turn over a new leaf? Give yourself up — Surrender and be a good man again?"

The man on the bed, looking a little surprised at the question, shook his head. Then he spoke bitterly.

"Today your father went to the farm where he was employed. He went to beg that the memsahib take him back on the farm. I don't know if he has returned yet. But my guess is that the memsahib struck him in the face and told him to clear off. The black man in his own country has been made into a dog. If we do not fight the situation will never be remedied."

I see, Karanja thought grimly. It sounds heroic. But all you blighters really do in the way of fighting is to burn villages and kill other black men. The other day at Lali you brutally murdered lots of innocent folk. Black folk... If you fellows had been educated you would certainly know better.

You have blood on your hands. If they come to shoot you it's a fair game. My father is a peace-abiding citizen and is not in this. Why should he die along with you? I have a soft spot for you but you must go...

"Uncle," Karanja said and stopped. His uncle's eyes were closed and he had fallen asleep. On his face was a look of pain, almost as if he had only closed his eyes and not sunk into peaceful slumber. For him sleep seemed not to unravel the worried sleave of care.

* * *

Mugo had decided against taking shelter in the old hut. For the two talking in the hut he had bad news. Ndonga had to leave in the night. It would be foolish and dangerous to let him stay any longer. God had kept the guards away. It was unlikely that He would help much longer. They had to come to their senses and help themselves.

Fresh trouble had broken out early that morning not very far from their home. The homeguards had been searching all day — and were still searching — for a gang of terrorists who had raided Bwana Eric Thomsett's farm. They had managed to kill a dog and mess up a few cows with simis. But Bwana Thomsett and his son had managed to hold them at bay until the security forces had come to the scene. The gang had melted away.

The memsahib's headman had told him the story when he had gone to the farm. Mugo had watched him closely. He was the headman: Could he have arranged to have him sacked?

"Thandi," he had said gravely, "Do you know why I lost my job?"

"No," Thandi had replied, "It was a great surprise to me. Since the memsahib's husband died she has not been herself. She has been very queer, you know. Now she sees in Mau Mau Fate's way of finishing her family off. She does not know which black man to trust. So she trusts nobody. Why she fired you I really do not know, but she has been rough with all of us. I believe if it were possible to run the farm without us she would do just that."

"It is a great curse, this Mau Mau." Mugo said. "But tell me, Thandi, is it wise to go to the memsahib and try to convince her of my innocence?"

"You cannot. At the mere sight of you she will be furious and might even strike you. You know the way their faces turn red like the eastern sky at dawn. (Have you got any snuff on you? ... Thank you). The memsahib has reached a point where if you annoy her greatly enough she could pull the trigger on you." Thandi slapped his own shot-gun affectionately.

Still I will try .... Mugo thought to himself. What can I do without my job. The garden might yield enough food for our stomachs *if* it rains well, but we need money for clothes and school fees. I wish this had come earlier — before I had built that new house with all my savings... But the memsahib might take me back — If I convince her of my innocence...

Innocence! Mugo sat up. For two nights he had harboured a dangerous gangster under his roof. That was enough to get a man hanged. What a fool he was! What a senseless, blundering fool he was to think of going to the memsahib! A search might be arranged in his house before the memsahib could take him back.

And Mugo would go to the gallows.

"What is the matter? You look frightened," Thandi said.

"No," Mugo replied.

"You know, if you really want to see the memsahib —"

"No!" Mugo replied.

Feeling sick he had taken leave of the headman. He had taken the path that led across the bridge to the rocks on the other side of the river. He had walked out of the memsahib's property with the sad heart of an exile. Somewhere high up on the rocks he had turned and looked back. The cattle, small moving specks in the distance were grazing down below. He had lain down on the rocks his face in his hands. He had not wept. He had slept.

* * *

They sat talking round the fire, his mother, father and sister. Karanja was deep in thought in a corner and did not talk much. The whole family had debated upon the fate of his uncle and had finally agreed to give him one more day. Karanja wondered what good that would do. As his uncle was not receiving any medical attention his leg was not improving at all; in fact it was getting worse. Although everybody wanted him to go they all lacked the courage to tell him to leave, seeing the condition he was in. His father was agitated, frightened — and helpless.

His mother and father discussed the family's future in hushed voices.

'We shall manage somehow," said his mother optimistically. "With the help of God we shall manage. Mugo, many years ago you were a craftsman. You used to make—"

"I can not go back to that, if that is what you are suggesting," Mugo said in alarm.

His wife served the food in silence. She was a tactful woman and never foolishly argued with her husband. She said, "Well, the Lord helps those who help themselves. In difficult times He doesn't drop manna from heaven as He did for the children of Israel.

"Certainly I shall look for work," her husband said defensively. "But I do not have very high hopes. All the Europeans are suspicious of any strangers and would hardly employ me just like that."

"But your old trade? Carpentry..."

"I failed in that. I cannot go back to it. The nights of hunger and misery still haunt me to this day. I can only work on a farm, Muthoni. That is the work I was made for."

Mugo sighed. Possibly he was thinking of the fine, sturdy cows he had left on the farm. The memsahib had entrusted them to his care and he had loved them almost as if they were his own. He understood cows and cows understood him. Many years back he had been born in a small hut many hills and valleys away. His earliest memories were linked with cattle for he had spent his boyhood looking after his father's herd. In those days, of course, you roamed all over the place looking for the best pasture for your cows. Provided your cows did not wander into someone's shamba nobody cared where they grazed. In those days grass was grass, and grass was for all. Life was never monotonous or precarious. There was companionship and lots of fun.

When his brother Ndonga was big enough he had helped him with the herd — and Mugo had taught him lots of boyish tricks. But they had had very few years together really and had never grown to understand each other When their father died Mugo had drifted into the city to look for fortune. Some years later his brother had followed but then Mugo, frustrated and disillusioned had left the city to work on a farm. From there to another farm where he had decided to remain permanently. Then of course *this*...

(Perhaps if their father had lived... But Ndonga had always been rather wild. It might not have changed things...).

Cows were cows, no matter who owned them — white or black. And Mugo had been as much at home with the memsahib's cattle as with his father's herd. Now he was like a fish that someone had seized from its water to examine in his hand. He lay in the hand of Fate, wondering into what sea he would find himself tossed next.

"Let us pray for the food," his wife's voice awakened him from his meditations. They all closed their eyes and she prayed. She thanked God for the food and then with increasing emotion asked Him to provide for them always in those dark times. Their lives had been thrown into a turmoil through which only His guiding hand had the power to lead them.

As she prayed Karanja in his corner opened his eyes and looked at them. No one was certain of the future any more...

He took two hot plates of food into the old hut. It was in darkness but after groping round in the darkness he found a match box on a stool and lit an oil lamp. Then he shook his uncle by the shoulder till he woke up with a violent start.

"What is it! What's happened?" said his uncle sitting up.

"I've brought your supper."

"It's you, Karanja," he said in great relief.

Karanja looked at him carefully. He observed a change in him from the afternoon. He looked tired and sick. And that softness seemed to have disappeared. What Karanja had seen the moment he had woken up with a start was a desperate wild man. A man with wild eyes, a wild face and wild stringy hair.

"Eat," Karanja said. He sat on one of the stones of the cold hearth and started on one of the plates. There was silence between them. But probably their thoughts were similar. Perhaps each was wondering what Fate held in store for him.

"It is cold in here," Karanja said. "Don't you feel it? Too bad mother finished up all the dry wood in the house. All the wood outside is wet. Curse this rain."

His uncle continued staring at the ceiling. Then he spoke. "It does not matter," he said.

Karanja looked down. It does not matter.... Karanja understood. In a short time his uncle would have to leave. Death no doubt awaited him, for with his leg he would not go far. What did a little warmth or food matter now?

"The wages of sin is death" his mother had said that evening. "When Ndonga came here staggering and bleeding in the leg he had probably murdered. There is nothing we can do for him, Mugo. Nothing whatsoever. He has killed and God saw it. We shall only be punished if we shelter him any longer."

All right, Karanja now thought, we might die for sheltering this man. He himself will die, I suppose. But for what? For fighting for his rights — or what he calls his rights. He is a fighter — an enemy of the memsahib and other white people. The memsahib has fired my father. Because of that all my dreams have come tumbling down because I know that there'll be no more school for me. My father can't afford the fees now. What a vicious little circle! I could complete it by killing the memsahib. That's an idea.

"Uncle," Karanja said, "That woman who shot you in the leg. What did you do to her?"

His uncle seemed to emerge from great depths. He did not turn.

"Let us not talk about it," he said rather curtly.

"Because uncle," Karanja went on, "There is one woman on my mind. She has spoilt my life. What hurts most is the thought that she does not even know what she has done to me. She merely pushed a little button as it were, and machines started to turn. A lot of things came tumbling down. She does not know every little thing that tumbled down. I'm one of the little things. She can't notice me because I am in the dust at her feet."

Slowly his uncle turned. His eyes glistened a little in the yellow light of the smoky lamp.

"The white memsaab?" he asked. His voice sounded dull and flat.

Karanja nodded. His uncle looked again at the ceiling.

"It is like that," he said at last, "when a little insect hums around you, intruding upon your calm and peaceful meditations you absent mindedly slap it against your leg, killing it. To the white race, we are insects. But Karanja, we have learnt to sting. So, my boy, sting. . . ."

Karanja stared at him for a moment.

"Well," he said, "I am really very upset, uncle. I don't know what to do with my life. My father was a carpenter when he was my age. He failed miserably. Mother says he should start again. Well I have been thinking. I could go into partnership with him. "Mugo and Son" sort of thing. Eat your food. It's getting cold. What do you think of the idea?"

His uncle made no reply.

"And do you know what we shall make if —" he stopped. His uncle was breathing quietly. He had fallen asleep again. He had not touched his food and Karanja thought of walking him. Then he thought better of it. He himself had hardly touched his food and had no appetite. He could understand his uncle not wanting food.

With his uncle asleep the hut was deathly quiet. The little smoky flame that lit up the hut flickered unsteadily. A sad feeling seized Karanja and suddenly he pushed his food away.

"Sting...." he said softly to himself. "If I knew it would serve any purpose I would sting...."

But Karanja felt that it would serve no purpose. Yes, it would complete the little vicious circle — but that would be all. Nobody's position would be improved. He would only become a hunted man like uncle Ndonga. He did not think that his uncle was a man to envy especially in his present situation.

Karanja ate as much as he could and then threw the rest of the food outside. With the plate he covered his uncle's food. Then he blew out the lamp and went out.

* * *

That night the rain poured gently on to the roof, and the sound lulled Karanja into slumber. But it was a troubled sleep. He dreamt that the homeguards had come to get his uncle. Everybody in the house was terrified as their footsteps came up to the house.

He woke up cold and frightened. He breathed a sigh of relief to find himself safe in his bed. He shook his head to disperse all memory of his dream, but to his surprise the footsteps persisted in his ears.

Karanja sat up in bed, his heart palpitating madly against his ribs. Terror seized him and choked him in the throat. It was no dream. There *were* footsteps!

The footsteps, he soon realised, belonged to one person and were receding slowly. Occasionally they sloshed in the mud heavily. Quietly, without making any sound Karanja got the window open and looked out. In the pale light of dawn he had a passing glimpse of a figure just before it staggered forward suddenly and disappeared through the wooden gate.

Karanja sighed again and closed the window. He smiled in the darkness. A drunkard who had missed his way, that was all, he decided. Still, he felt rather weak.

Afterwards he often wondered what would have been the outcome had he stuck to his conclusion and gone back to sleep and not been struck, as he was a few minutes later, by the strangeness of it all — the idea of a drunkard at that hour. A sickening idea occurred to him and he got out of bed hurriedly. He put on a pair of shorts and his school pullover and went out of the house. The mud was thick and soft and his shoes sank disgustingly into it. He reached the hut and knocked upon the door. When there was no answer from within he pushed the door open.

He was not very surprised to find his uncle gone.

* * *

Thandi, the headman stirred out of bed. It was early for only one cock had crowed. He went outside and contemplated the world. It had really rained. He did not expect the terrorists had been able to carry out any plans they might have had for the night. If it always rained like that — but then every gangster would secure for himself a raincoat.

In the east the sky had cleared somewhat. It was the colour of blood. On the whole it looked like a fine day.

Thandi yawned and stretched. Then he went back inside to start the fire and make some tea. The children were not going to school today for the holidays had begun and so his wife would sleep for another hour or so. He himself could not afford to wake up late. He had a job to do. The memsahib would not tolerate laziness or slackness from her number one man.

To wake up in the morning these days gave him great relief. Sleep was no longer a pleasure. You slept in fear and dread of what might creep out of the night. You dreamt dreams that left you cold and shaken. To wake up and find that Mau Mau had not set the whole camp ablaze and that you still had your neck gave you a warm feeling in your insides...

As the water warmed up on the fire he went to the bed and carefully, so as not to disturb his wife, pulled out his shot gun. He loved this gun. One day, he was sure, it would save his life. It was his practice to clean it every morning.

He had just sat down to start his work when he heard a sound outside the hut followed by footsteps. His grip tightened on the gun. All his senses were at once alert. Could it be....? Not so early in the morning really. Not in broad daylight....

But the headman was not taking any chances. He stood waiting, his gun ready.

There was a knock. A rather hesitant knock that somehow made his muscles relax a little.

"Who is it?" he asked.

"It is me — Karanja," said a breathless voice.

Thandi smiled to himself. This time at least there was no trouble. But there were times when he wished it would come and be done with. This waiting — for heaven knew what — was getting into his nerves.

Karanja stood waiting outside. He shot uneasy sideways glances at his uncle fearing he might fall. But he looked a little better. At least he could stand without support.

He had caught up with him halfway down the hill near the labourers quarters. He could have caught up with him earlier but that had not been the idea. He had followed his uncle, on discovering that he had left the hut, out of curiosity. To his amazement his uncle had not bothered to keep to the bush. He had hobbled quickly along the road, staggering in a manner painful to watch. The crazy fool would not get far, Karanja thought.

Yet he could not run up to him and beg him to come back...

Quickly, like one with a purpose, his uncle had struggled along the muddy road. Then suddenly he had rushed into the bushes and hurled himself into the interior, and Karanja could see his head and shoulders as he desperately penetrated the rich growth of marigolds.

Karanja, feeling sick at the sight, had followed. Now he wanted to reach his uncle, though what there was to tell him he was not certain.

His uncle had left the bushes and stumbled upon a path. Perhaps he knew where he was going, Karanja thought. Perhaps he had a friend around here. Karanja felt happy at the thought. Then his uncle had fallen.

He had clung to a wayside shrub and dragged himself inside it, crawling in the dust. Karanja had watched with a bleeding heart and then run forward.

"I'm home! I am home...!"

The words, made with breathless gasps seemed to cut the thick tense silence of dawn and hang heavily in the atmosphere.

"Uncle," Karanja called as he walked up.

His uncle took no notice of him. He was busy trying to make himself comfortable inside the shrub. All the time he talked incoherently to himself. He was not mad, Karanja knew. He was just sick and delirious.

He had crept deep inside the wet shrub and snuggled in there, no doubt in the belief that he was home. The feel of the wet leaves on his face and the scratching of the twigs must have overwhelmed him. He had started to whimper. The sound was unpleasant and sickening.

Talking was futile, Karanja soon realised. With sudden determination he had seized him by the legs and dragged him from the shrub. Then he had looked down at the labourers' camp down below.

Down there his uncle could rest — even if it was to await one of those quick trials that always seemed to lead, for people such as he, invariably to the hangman's noose. The game was up for Ndonga, freedom fighter.

* * *

When the door opened a man stood in the shadows, framed in the doorway. For a moment he peered at those standing outside. Then he made a noise in his throat. The gun in his hand spurted flame, leaping and roaring in his hand.

Karanja sat up. Strange that he felt no pain and was alive. He listened to the throbbing in his heart. An acrid whiff of smoke came to his nostrils. All the time he stared at the man in the shadows — and the gun that was pointed down at him.

To his ears came the sound of excited voices and hurrying feet that squelched in the mud. He was in the mud himself and the water soaked through his pants. He tried to move. His hand rested on something soft... An arm behind him. Suddenly he did not care about the mud and the water anymore.

"Karanja . . ." The man in the shadows said. Somehow he was a stranger now. He sounded astonished and incredulous. . .

Karanja looked round at the beginning of a crowd. His head seemed to swim. His mouth had already dried up. A sharp panic shot through him. He turned to the headman in desperation and opened his mouth to speak, to lie, to plead, to . . . .

The headman's eyes had left his face and turned to the still, prostrate figure behind Karanja. A little smile of satisfaction came to his lips. He addressed a little boy in the gathering crowd.

"Go and call the memsahib," he said.

eight

1954

April morning steals in slowly round the corner, rolls out back lane. Sun sneaks hand through clouds, brushes a sinister finger roughly along the squalid alley. It's eight o'clock; you and I can hear some bell. Being still half asleep, unready for mankind, Sun rolls back to bed into a grey bush of ragged clouds. To the city below, the potent waste is an angry jungle which weighs there quivering, binding time, ready. After surveying the scene below ("it always shines later, memsahib"), darts of rain begin to fire. Catches them, pedestrians, uncovered. Catches them, beggars, unaware. The war is on.

Hastily, the beggars — uncomplaining — wipe their eyes on the back of the hand or the tattered sleeve, in an attempt to come to terms with the new day, while those with legs dance toe against toe, to rub in some warmth and tickle the jigger. They crawl out back lane, beat at flies following in their wake, yawn, stretch what limb can be said to stretch, and being good Christians search the new day and God.

Rain. Rain all over the beggars' pavement, rain seeking pools in gutters, rain rushing rivulets. Rain upon the pedestrian ladies and gentlemen who brushed aside the weather report, rain reaching out for the hawkers and jetsam who never heard of weather reports. Downpour: drums hard on all April fools who are glad hot March has gone to bed last night, a clown's smile curved at lip's edge. Rain: seeking fools in these begging seekers of God who should know better than embrace a wet morning joke with nothing but browned rags for cover and 'Give us this day our bread . . .' murmured on drooping lips.

Beyond, the roof harbouring the Governor of the Colony and his jamaa hums a very peaceful mocking bird buzz. Further afield, in the industrial quarter, the early factory chimney, there, yonder, you fool! bursts one hell of a smoky kick into the heavenly clouds above, and beaten, joins them. Amen. The volkswagen arrested and lonesome in the traffic-jam like a bead on a string shakes in anger, its posterior coughing — sickly — at the morris behind . . . Beggar anonymous take warning to cross the street on all fours at this time of all times is hardly intelligent: it holds business and stirs anger thank you, damn you, there will be plenty of time for that. Couldn't keep on the pavement if people didn't work, now could he? Time they got them off to some institution too. Could learn some useful trade, you know. Weaving, carving. A certain amount of laziness, no doubt. Take cleanliness, sir. They could kind of washup, honest to God. Great responsibility, sir, this alms shauri . . .

Rain. Rain over the street of responsibility, the responsible-fors and the liabilities. And the angry bush above seems to weigh darker and darker. Big muscular drops vibrate on windscreen like scattered crystal beads connecting only to disconnect. Vision gets blurred and that's . . . enough reason to clear that liability off under the tyre some riddance too poor man god rest his soul. Don't know to cross Delamere Avenue than can shoot straight these maumau. Nearly maiming drivers too at the East African Safari, two-pound rocks from behind the bushes more risk than skiing Kilimanjaro, sir . . .

Sun strokes the street with palm of the hand, beggars clear their throats and spit — right out there on the pavement — while able-bodied Kamau corners into back lane umbrella in one hand and, legs askew, fumbles with his fly. Sun quickly withdraws hand, seeing it's all saliva and wet and zips: and the rain comes down over again . . . It's going to be rough today old man Cynthia said so and Cynthia should know. Man how that woman knows. Went out the night before the night before you know what I mean and when I got home she said do you know what time it is Charlie Walker Mr. Charles Walker d'you know what time it is. Three o'clock love I said then she rolled over and turned her back on me and I could tell she knew I knew she knew where I'd been. Charlie she said an hour later. Love? Oh never mind. But I did mind. You couldn't stagger home at the crack of dawn and not mind at least not to Cynthia if I know her these twenty years. Not when you've been out with the boys talking native women and marital bliss. Seems rough on the side too you know what I mean . . . the neighbourhood saw poor Smith back home so fast the other day he couldn't appeal to his cricket side.

Rain. Red traffic light. Beggar anonymous crawls across. Couldn't have heard of zebra crossings . . . Most unproductive, sir. Can't tell the genuine from the humbugs escaping from the villages. There's hell in the villages, I tell you. I mean when old Briggs there's got a woman talks faster than a machine gun he's bound to go give hell to some sinner besides if he didn't join what would *they* say you tell me. Take the other 'noon the wife had the girls to tea. Mrs. McPherson cackled what Charles in bed? my Blair had a bad cold in bed I told him the villages will do *him* good perhaps you ought to get Charles up tell him there's no telling what these people will do to us women if all husbands are in bed with a slight cold as if just thinking about Kimathi isn't enough. And would you believe it sir all the wives agreed Cynthia rush to the bedroom shake me up by the moustache go connect the bayonet at any dark target before the whole side is wiped out on account of some malingering hubby. So I snored like I never snored these past twenty years of marital bliss sir and whisker or no whisker I wouldn't come alive and out of bed ready to shoot any blinking witching raping native no sir not for all the chaste wives in the blinking neighbourhood no. But are we in this business sir? Man, we've been fleeing them updown backfront they don't know whether they're going or coming by God have we! I'm on the reserve you see. Farming one thousand acres during the day, beautiful soil... But look at those clouds sir, look at that big black fellow hanging out there and tell me truly if it pretends any good to my coffee sir. The way the old man sends rain when no coffee-bean cares a drop just pisses you off. Precisely why I don't go to church any more sir, precisely why... Heck nobody's going to cough verily verily I say unto ye all over a glass of good water and fool me it's wine fresh from the Father's vineyard; mass hypnotism I tell you, native stuff too ask Lathbury but does it keep them from going into the forest and doing the quickstep all over the fig tree? Look out of the window sir see that bowtie; there's the Sunday school exterior for you sir but the Lord bless us maumau from top to bottom and back again. Shoot off their legs I say so they confess ... We'll park, we'll park, this is the land of bado kidogo... shoot off their legs. Rider Haggard would have said that if his English was good enough but the last I saw of books girl called Lessing was contradicting Allan Quartermain; just fancy that sir and I'll tell you she's not the last either: sir, would you take this from yet another cheap-jack — sticks round the corner on one leg arms folded eating bubblegum tells you he's angry and come to save the world from christ philistines and tories to hell with everybody everybody stinks. Spoilt kids I say spoilt kids. Can't count enough teeth to chew bubblegum only shaggy hair and sex I could whip the lot trust me I would. Shoot their legs off! Any day too spoilt kids. Send them over man and they won't tickle under the seat any more because nobody's laughing no sir not Charles Walker no sir I'll show them who's angry ... This is the formula to lose Kenya — upstarts... add bubblegum... I hate bubblegum....

Rain. Showers singing. Singing overhead, occasionally gushing in the wind to disturb the pavement and the beggars and their talk. Singing now a sad tune up on the roof above, now perhaps a happier one, but always the swing of the strain to the plea of Give us this day our daily bread for we still believe, palms outstretched as of an idiot boy who expects the answer to fall from heaven and therefore deserves a splash of the ruler by the bush Teacher who couldn't care half a calabash about arithmetic anyhow. Rain. God's splash in this godless city, Noah's flood to see who wears the pants in this country of the pharisees. But the pedestrian gentlemen who forgot their umbrellas only swear hell at the old man upstairs and the neat ladies bear it nicely saying this is a fine way to win men's hearts indeed. Rain. Comes down with all the fury of its indifference, even malice, Charles Walker swears something about his doomed coffee as he drives round, beggars wail something about their daily trespasses, and Kamau retreats into yet another back lane to let fly his fly. Well-to-do Philipino Augustus Njage, Esq., lifts his bowler hat to scratch a lone patch, swings along. 'You keep coming back like a song' or something like that whistled on dry lips. Justin or Justino Christian Omolo Mboya, native-american-agitator-almost-communist, walks hatless like a truly oppressed, perseveres beads of water on his beard. Narain N. Singh must protect turban by holding hot mau mau news in the 'Standard' above his head and knows it's going to be news indeed for how does one play Pakistan next Sunday up to the hockey stick in mud? And out there across this very street lonely Mrs. Powdermaker whose everybody's PRO Mr. Powdermaker bought her a new raincoat at last on Mrs. Powdermaker's nagging stops halfaminute to admonish Mr. Martin in one breath for reading the dreadful weather report on the radio what's more walking out uncovered himself what's more saying this weather what's more unchivalrously letting Mrs. Martin catch her morning of cold in a raincoat fashionable in Paris five summers ago as if rain did not work in more ways than one its wonder through tears in old coats to perform what's more etcetera. On the pavement, two beggars:

— April the first — bad start, says the first.

— What? asks the second. I wonder you have nothing better to do than keep count of the year. Raining jiggers under the buttocks and you have the warm breath to lie there and say to me, it's April today. Bugs! I hate time.

— There you go crawling all over me now. What's in saying it's April today? What's your sullen mother anyway?

A man can't crawl here night upon day and not touch breaths about something. If I were to say that your temper buries away every sunset and it is as if I am to answer for it the way you shout at me the next morning what would you say? You would only crack: 'Jiggers! you split your head again last night walking in another of your bad dreams!' Well, I have nothing against walking. I used to in and out of my bad dreams before they shot my legs off in the forest. In fact —

— What's the matter Ngure, Ngure, Ngure! Keep your bottoms down. One small breath from me and you lead me into the bush of the forest once again. Well, they shot your legs off but you killed somebody didn't you? Now, god or whoever it was shot my legs off before my sullen mother bore me and I couldn't very well shoot his legs off, can I? How is it that the whole street must know we are at it again? It's not as if you beg from them the way you dance and split bottoms all over the pavement. Talk of sullen mothers!

— March, April, May... Look, I count the year for the same reason you call me bugs and jiggers — to keep warm my lips. Else if I thought you meant I was bugs and rats I'd knock you a good one on the calabash.

— You try, son of an affluent mother. Stretch your arm or you will be borrowing from me again...

— August, September...

— If you must talk talk Christmas! It is the only time that matters. Strangers flock to the city and then you don't have to stretch your April arm half the day for nothing.

— New year's day is also good.

—Oh, termites, what's the difference! It is all Christmas is it not? Stop taking advantage of me you standard-four and all that. Impotent goat! Must you split the year every time you yawn...

— Did you say impotent goat? Listen you son of a catholic priest hear me, I have a son you know...

— Ho, ho!... the idiot boy. You are proud of him are you not? Broken pot of a head who couldn't save his own mother when the home guards came. And looking up and down this street I don't think he had to take after a lot of people either.

— I said I'd knock you a good one, see here!

— Phooey!

— April too early for the rain or too late? I have lost count. Now, nothing good comes of April; I should strike it off my fingers. But how do you make up for it...

—...add another moon, you fool. Why don't you try the stars for a change?

— There are no stars. They are behind that bush, laughing, I tell you laughing, can't you hear? Besides, last time counting them back lane my head swam round and round the night stars sang in my eyes spirits flew all over ears like a swarm of bees and God said you are a silly little man daring the universe with all his sins who gets shot before he can free his country now begs money from those who shot him so He would fire rain and hell and punish me for my sins throw me to my ancestors who are cannibals and uneducated so I was forced by my maumau oath number seven to tell Him He is the sinner the way He took away Gikuyu na Mumbi's country all for salt, the swindler, and now leaves me to fight His missionary in difficult bush conditions He would see who has a sharper spear the God of Kirinyaga or Himself... But came the dawn and you converted me again you fool.

— Try the cars then and don't you talk like that to me Ngure. Sometimes I think you ought to have been a politician.

— I am. April, thirty days, May — forget it; it would make more sense spelt backwards. June.... thirty two?

— Try the cars countryman, anything, but change the subject. You'll be sending me to Mathare next. Count your fingers if you like...

— I can count beyond twenty! But you, your mind grows nasty and rusty because you cannot count. It clears the mind you know. I ask you, why don't you try counting beyond ten? Connects the beads, you know...

— I'll say it does!

— It is like extending the universe within yourself.

— Listen you people! What does one hear next — you would stop yawning and extend that wrinkled stomach to the right belly if you would only work harder and damn the universe. See how they pass you by. I don't care if your abdomen caves in your back with hunger, just let me catch your hand in my pockets again tonight Ngure.

— Have you ever been alone with the full moon, with the universe; alone in the quiet of the forest?... Have you? ... It is calm.... dark... not a breeze; and not a soul. You've been lost in the forest since twilight, daylight's behind you. You suffered great casualties and as soon as General Kairu was killed you lost hope. You lose hope and escape. Alone. You can hear others still fighting to their last oath, death. But you convince yourself that everybody has run away from the growing dark, including the white soldiers who have perhaps sent a radio call for more cannon fodder from the King's African Rifles. You tell yourself the government forces will probably wait until early next morning anyway or they will miss the whores in Nyeri town — and you could do with one yourself. So, wounded, self-convinced, you congratulate yourself, and seek safety. Run. Run, run, for miles it matters not where. But you run alone. Then weak, you finally lie down. It is lonely running alone... The forest is thin here, your mind in peace; war is not here. It's strange. Your arm has stopped hurting, provided you don't move it. The bandage is wet, sticky with your blood. You are laid like a log. Strangely, you feel your mind turn over the wooden years, back, back, and turning, you feel it touch upon soft waters somewhere, somewhere around the Past. It is peaceful here. Nothing can reach you. Then, Silence gains in on you. Unearthly sounds are loose upon your ears. But it's calm, no breeze. You are at peace, thank Ngai. But you can't sleep. More silence gains on you, furiously, the fury of ghostly insects wringing and twitching and squealing at your ears, mind. The flesh-and-blood woman curved in the moon holds baby Jesus sadly, looks at Unpredictable Silence, hard god on the face of innocence. You question. Stars tear in and out of the dark of your eyes like pins, the unearthly insects prick at your ears sharper than sound. You are laid like a dog. Again you dare? Then somewhere in the mind's waste you are no longer on your back, you stand upright. You try to turn your face, to clutch at the tree nearest you, to feel you are this side of ghosts and ancestors. But you can't. The nearest tree starts to move and you can't even shoot at it with your home-made gun because you are a tree yourself, you can't even turn. You call upon Ngai. He laughs aloud. You call upon God. He spins and grows out of the face of the moon at the apex of your mind's universe and laughs a meteorite way into Ngai's arms. They join forces, merge into one Great Silence, closing in on the limits of your mind. Your legs have grown root, you feel your body going down, down, and you can't even grow up. Lost like a child, you are being buried, you can't think or hit back or scream I hate you God because trees cannot hit back, they only fall. You are up to the neck, mouth, head, gone; alone. Gone, gone, and buried, and small, and wriggling roots with other trees, being licked for water. Listen... they are better than you because they can still breathe they can still see, they can't say 'why'. But you can... So you fight the Silent Battle, scream within yourself and there isn't a soul to save you. 'Why me?' And because you escaped alone, you fight alone; suffocated in the depth, wriggling, ridiculous, no doubt forgotten. You try to count. One swims into two, two into three, three into forfisix, forfisix into an obscene tune in the distant whores' town. You try again. Somewhere in the waste of your tree's mind Great Silence laughs aloud, says: 'You are a silly little maumau. You will die alone, alone you will rot — and no carcass of a tree or man comes up here either. Your soul you can keep or if you will I shall grow more trees with. Goodbye and don't forget those songs of praise.' You try to force fourfisix into seneighnine, a dry mouth echoes at some end but you finally heave over the thirsty pangs of eighnineten and Eleven takes shape, the shape of two hooded trees, gate-out in Ngai's dry cemetery. Then out of His nowhere dark, Great Silence flickers into a myriad stars singing in your eyes and a great ball spins small, takes shape. It's the moon. You lick your dry tongue all over the curved-in woman of flesh-and-blood thirtyfour-thirtyfive-thirtysix; counting to keep counting. You feel humbled like a tree, silly. Then... you wake up, knock your stupid head against a tree, take your home-made gun and say: 'Saint Peter Saint Peter, you stinker...' Your mind is clean, organised.

— Wake up Ngure, who was it this time — King Elithabeth herself?

— I just fell asleep.

— You are always falling asleep. Only, let me catch hands in my pockets tonight and some idler will see stars . . .

Rain. Rain on the street of begging liability, liability on the street of unzipping gentlemen. Clouds are dark: here and there iced ash-white, burnt-out; there and here blotting black like clotting blood. They suspend silently above the skyscraper, like an immense stalactite of soot weighed down our collapsing thatch roof. In and out of the wet of the urinating town Man ventures good morning to Man:

Cabbages, ma'am? Is it not more bad than Englishman's weather? *Who said that? I wouldn't have said that, what d'you take me for?* Do you love me by this very bible Wanjiru? *Hold me, everybody hold me or I'll kill him!* Hold him everybody hold him so I can kill him! *Will man find peace in this world? I mean, hardly are you in bed than her plait-haired husband staggers home from the forest and says he is lonely — I actually broke his neck . . .* Trust to the Lord, trust to the Lord *Leftright leftright leftright . . .* A raise, my foot! What do you blacks think the Company is, a mint? *Hey, you what's rain to do with pressed bowels zip-up!* You unchristian muslims!

Parasites! Every man run alone, I always say I see you have come to borrow from me again *Metropole? my wife doesn't have to know* Remember me for uhuru. . . I know uhuru is to come some day distant . . . deport me? . . . Throw me where? . . . I — I don't even know where river Ganges is! . . . present for bibi, bwana . . . pay me? Why you pay me now? Friendship possible, no? *. . . This native weather . . . typical!* You are being highly misunderstanding me completely . . . *mummy, is two plus two four . . .*

Rain. Charles Walker takes another look at that black fellow hanging out there, walks his mind through his nicely laid lines of coffee, adds two plus two, gets three, breaks down. And down comes the rain, merrily, merrily, ('Allah be praised, rain at last') and down drains the talk of rats paving pavements:

— *All* Fools Day, today...

— Oh, rats! who cares... you and I have got to move houses Ngure. I can't bear you.

— We have no houses. If there are twelve months...

— We will move pavements then!

—Right, let's move. Here I am trying to count so I can tell next Boxing Day and you keep interrupting saying all December is Christmas and rich tourists and I tell you there is only one week that matters for Christmas and I repeat with all wise men that there is only one week that counts for Christmas and you dare contradict me! All right then, crawl off.

— You ought to be ashamed of yourself.

— I am. Losing my legs like that, now begging from them. Strike a day off April's tail...

— Cockroaches!

— Hey, what's all this cockroaches and termites, you fool?

— Nothing old warrior... nothing....

— There are three hundred and sixty five days running...

nine

the tailor

"What you want?" he demanded.

He studied the youth long and hard. Blood-shot eyes; haggard face. Spirals of unkempt hair. Stained collar. Like the inside of a chocolate paper. That read as much of shop-lifting as anything else.

"I'm looking for a job," Njogu answered. "Any kind of job."

But Mr. Shah knew better than that. Too many people hang around his shop looking for jobs these days, he said to himself. The net result was that somehow or other, things disappeared. That is, money disappeared. And in his forty years of hard tailoring, money was the one lesson Mr. Shah had learnt, and would preserve.

He had seen hard times. But it did seem to many that the major incidents of his life had only served to jolt him up higher steps and that the struggle up the ladder had not been as insurmountable as he loved to tell. Forgetting his bad moments in youth, he never reflected on those early days to identify his plight then with that of the numerous haggard faces brown or black who called to ask, or more often than not beg, him to take them in.

He had come from India at the age of fifteen owing to his adventurous bent and the fact that he stood little chance at home. In awe, he had watched his brothers thrown out one after the other onto the streets, in the grim struggle for survival. But Shah wanted to *live*. As is the nature of Man, the population explosion made no sense to his parents. Providence had seen mankind through in the past, so be it in the future. They went on multiplying.

Mamdani Halji Karamjee Shah was the fourteenth, and by no means the last.

As soon as he reached the age of fifteen and saw the street of grim prospects beckoning him, Shah stole away in a dhow. He was eighty-four days at sea. Rats ate his food, the Monsoon sun boiled down in humid cruelty and water, in conspiracy, ran scarce. Nevertheless, he successfully came to grips with these. He shook hands with Circumstances and said, 'I am fasting'.

More by passive endurance than any optimistic action, the sun-baked crew eventually drifted ashore. Shah himself landed with the air of a sea-sick explorer and adventurer at Mombasa Port.

Despite the Man-Eaters of Tsavo, he managed to hitch-hike his way into Nairobi. Luck was with him, and the Town Council gave him a job as Health Inspector. This meant that with his head buried under a large Chinese hat to ward off the sun, as Supervisor he had to see that there were no orange peels lying about the street, or dustbins which remained full and stinking.

Those, for him, were the trying days of Nairobi Town in the dust. For the sun, more often than not, came down dust-yellow. No one had yet come up with the idea of macadamising the streets; or in fairness to those town fathers, the streets were then not much of streets, anyway, and did not warrant macadamising just because, as Shah loved to say in later years, some people rode in rickshaws. Those were indeed the days of Shah Barefoot, Shah Nearstarvation and Shah Sickforhome.

Ten years later, he found he had had quite enough walking up and down Bazaar Street. He therefore considered it timely that an ageing pioneer and distant cousin should offer him a chance in the tailoring trade and he duly took his premises in "Halbi Mansion, C/o Halbi Proprietors, Government Road, Nairobi."

Sooner or later, his benefactor died. As it was only natural that one man's loss should be another's gain, Shah was not surprised, as the only relation this side of the Indian Ocean, to find himself willed the shop. The spirit and enthusiasm with which the beneficiary embraced his good fortune, however, could only be interpreted as that the old man had not died a thread-and-needle too soon. In print bold and glaring, Shah immediately put outside his shop: M. H. K. SHAH, TAILOR AND OUTFITTER — *WELCOME.*

All other signs had comfortably taken shelter behind dust to a degree of virtual illegibility. The tide of customers flowed into his shop.

For the next fifteen years, Shah's tape-measure went up, down and round, among others, the Kenya Colony's Governor, the Aga Khan, and visiting English gentry come to the Tropics for sunshine, hunting and convalescence: or merely to see at its savage proximity, Africa's roaring wild and to write home about it. The fashion of the day in short, fell under the pedal of M. H. K. 's sewing machine. You could easily pick out in a crowd, a Shah jacket, a Shah pair of pants, or a Shah school blazer.

This paid dividends in that besides now weighing 210 pounds M. H. K. gained a string of other shops. It also gave him the satisfied feeling that the runaway sheep of the family had become its saviour. He sent home fifty rupees a week.

Now so many years later, at the time of Njogu's suspicious and certainly impudent entry, he was sending home £50, for which he was signing a cheque.

* * *

The year was 1954 and the cold of a July morning which he poorly braved with a khaki shirt, pants and bare feet, had been sprinkled, like the brown dirt in his clothes, into every corner, into every employer, into the heart of humanity. He turned round into Government Road. The problem was not really the choice of place for his next call. Here it was, the biggest tailoring shop in Nairobi. Its doors, wide-open arms, flung him a warm invitation.

He stood at the edge of the pavement. He looked up and down the street to the last car in traffic. His hesitant, jumpy manner betrayed that the marvels of the City had taken yet another reserve dweller breathless. At last he sprinted across.

He stopped, shivering at the display window, undecided whether to step in or go and call elsewhere. But considering his luck so far, the tailor's shop was as good as elsewhere. He looked inside. Its vast, full interior contrasted its tidiness on his shabby clothes and defied him to enter. He had his eyes on the contents behind the glass window when somebody flanked a voluminous frame against him with an imposing aura of ownership.

"What kind of job you want?" Mr. Shah asked as he signed the cheque. "You have qualification, no?"

"Any kind of job," Njogu repeated. "I reached Standard Six." He might have added that his parents were killed in the Emergency. But looking up into Mr. Shah's eyes, he wondered whether this was a sentimental qualification.

"No job. No job at all for your qualifications." Mr. Shah leant back in his chair. Cold, hard silence settled in the air except for vehicles breaking dangerously out on the streets.

It seemed to Njogu that this vast place which everyone in the reserve warned against, would in time swallow him up naked, mercilessly, and he was afraid.

The big shops stood proud. It was not as if they shared amongst them a secret history of the dusty and muddy times they had once known alongside the streets they flanked. No, it was as if they could be touched no more. The vulnerability of the streets had gone, and with the clean murram, as with the full tempting glass windows, had come a certain ease and hardness of heart in everything, everybody. To-day there were only two kinds of humans in the money-grabbing Nairobi society: those who continuously stepped on other people's toes and those who had theirs continuously stepped upon. Both were unanimous on the evils of having theirs stepped upon. But given a fair chance, each would still readily raise their feet.

Njogu wanted to run out, finish it off under the tyres of the indifferent vehicles. But he didn't. He stood there.

He must not be disheartened. Had not his aunt said, "Try them thrice, begthembegthembegthem! thrice before you give up"?

"How old you are?" asked Mr. Shah, turning to his lunch time news broadcast on the Asian Service.

He would be fourteen next week or rather his parents would be dead one month then. Only people told him he looked too big for his age; his father had died fighting in the forest, his mother had been shot by the Mau Mau at home. Njogu could do nothing but run to the City to his aunt. Masa Karoki was long widowed and it was she in fact who seemed to need help. She was frail and sick. She could not afford to keep him or herself, so would Mr. Shah —

Mr. Shah banged his fist on the table and said he had heard enough. He stood up. He ran his hands up and down his trousers braces. He played his body on the balls of his feet. Then, loudly, he announced that the government tapped him at the rate of tens of pounds in tax each year and if anyone needing his help would go rescue it off the government the pleasure was very much Mr. Shah's. He had no job for Mau Mau.

Njogu said that he was not; that he did not know what Mau Mau was. He knew that his father went to the forest to fight for a cause. He cursed his wife for not going out with him and died there. She prayed for him for going out into the forest and died at home. Both were gone and —

He stopped and looked at Mr. Shah. Mr. Shah stared at his radio set and the wanted youth in quick, unbelieving alternation . . .

> *The woman Masa Karoki died soon on reaching the hospital. The motive of the crime is unknown, although the police have reason to believe that this is another in a series of savage, cold-blooded murders that have been accurring in Nairobi. It is believed that the killer of Masa Karoki, an old woman who has been bed-ridden for some months is Kikuyu, and not more than twenty . . .*

Kikuyu, and not more than twenty . . .

Mr. Shah fetched his whistle.

...An eye witness said that he was barefooted and very shabby looking. The police are anxious to get anyone who can give more information. Please contact Kingsway Police Station or ...

Mr. Shah cursed. Was he not being irresponsible? Here was his chance to show Mr. Jones the police inspector that far from being among the "cowardly bunch of shopkeepers who let Mau Mau breed", he stood by the law. Besides, there was a prize. He turned to Njogu.

"They have not caught you yet?"

He must not let the youth run away. That would be a fine kettle of fish indeed. Inspector Jones scared him. His bushy moustache was enough to send any tailor up the wall. Jones would be the last inspector to have his men go on a wild goose chase. *If you catch a Mau Mau you must hold him and call for help.*

Suddenly, Njogu remembered. "They have not caught you yet?" He was scared. Earlier that morning the soldiers had swept Kikuyu men and boys off the City taking them to Langata Camp for screening. He had hidden under a parked vehicle in a back lane. Now Mr. Shah had used the telephone. Was it for the police? If he couldn't get a job, at least he could still dash out.

* * *

Brakes whined, screeched; split-second pain and scream. Loud, helpless cry. Like a fourteen year old. Then, blankness. Sprinkles of blood on windscreen. Cars swerved. Everything, everyone, stood still. A crowd began to gather round the sprawled body.

"He is dead," someone said.

"No he will live," said another.

Njogu stood across the street, flanked by two policemen. Stunned, he had been unable to run away to his aunt, Masa Karoki. He found it hard to believe the reality, the actual being of a man only a while ago, a man who had looked so powerfully intimidating as he chased him, shouting, blowing his whistle. He was now helpless; perhaps dying, at best maimed. An island of loneliness, he lay only encircled by a group of people with hard, urban faces which registered more curiosity than emotion. And it might well be, Njogu thought sadly, that in that rough hour of unexpected pain, Mr. Shah did after all need him, did need someone, anyone.

"He is dead," a woman cried.

Njogu rubbed the back of his dirty hand up and down his cheek. The street around him had suddenly gone blank and unreal in his mind. After a moment, he wiped his face again. He did not know why he felt concerned. True, Mr. Shah had handled him roughly. But as he lay gripped between the two policemen he could only wonder if that's how close death could be, and he felt tears well down his cheek, inarticulately. Falling quietly, as if telling a very personal story, perhaps one of a kind of bond in suffering, nevertheless softly falling.

"Let's go, you young hound!"

Njogu stole a last look towards the prostrate body across the street.

ten

the last breath

We watched Eva walking firmly back to her dormitory. I glanced sideways at Dad. He was watching her with a strange, tense look in his eye.

I hesitate on the word "tense," doubtful as to whether Dad was ever tense in his life. But the look in his eye was very strange as he watched her walk away.

I wondered what he was thinking. Whatever it was it made no difference. I loved Eva and would marry her as soon as I possibly could.

Suddenly, without a word Dad started the engine and drove furiously down the road towards the gate of the blind school.

"What will you do? You can't marry her like that!" he shouted above the roar of the engine.

I looked at him swiftly. His eyes were steady on the road. Anger flooded through me. So the visit had been in vain. So he had seen nothing of the inner Eva.

"We've gone through all this before," I said. "Now you have seen her. My last word on the subject is this. When I come of age next August I am going to ask Eva to marry me."

"But she is blind . . . !"

I sank back in my seat. This was hopeless. For how long would Dad keep on beating home the fact? As if it wasn't home already — and what was more, accepted!

"Then give her eyes," my voice was hoarse with anger.

A look of surprise momentarily came to Dad's face. Then he looked grim. Though he didn't seem to realise it he increased his speed. I thought I knew what had got hold of Dad, and the thought brought a faint smile on to my lips.

Dad was confused and angry with himself for it. He had until now thought of Eva as a blind, helpless creature who had stolen my heart. Now he had seen her and perhaps caught a glimpse of the angel in her — and had even seen, perhaps, how very far from helpless Eva was.

"What are you going to do?" I asked in a shout, for now the mad roar of the car would have drowned anything less.

Dad didn't reply. A terrible cough shook his frame and the car swerved dangerously to the edge of the road.

He corrected this (just in time too!) and settled comfortably in his seat.

Neither of us talked again till we got back home. I left the car silently and entered the house. I went to my room and sank on to my bed with a sigh.

I wondered bitterly when my father would start to understand me and my feelings.

It seemed to me that our ideas had always clashed ever since I had been a kid. There seemed little in my past life that I could heartily thank him for. Time and again he had interfered with my plans. Only a year before he had ruined a plan I had to study music. Thus I had ended up in a bank and was likely to remain there for a long time.

That he always meant well I never doubted. But I was equally sure I knew what was best for me. Dad would make no more decisions for me; I loved Eva and would marry her in the near future, and take care of her.

Mother entered the room cautiously and interrupted my rather impassioned line of thought.

"Well, how did it go?" She asked in a good attempt to sound lighthearted. But I could tell she was very serious, deep inside.

Mother understood me. She had met Eva some weeks back and had liked her very much. Although she hoped I would change my mind about it all — marriage, that is — she understood my feelings and never tried to argue me out of it.

"He met her," I said heavily; "it made little difference to him." I paused to consider this. At least he is still very stubborn. But I'll show him I have a mind of my own!" I finished a little savagely.

"Yes, but be careful!" Mother looked alarmed, "He looked so dark — and troubled. . ."

"What does he say? Mother," I pleaded suddenly seized by a wave of feeling and passion, "Why don't you say you understand? Of course I wish Eva could see, but just because she can't, through no fault of her own, it shouldn't make Dad regard her as an outcast. She says I have brought sunshine in to her life. Think of that mother. If I left her I'd plunge her back into darkness. . ." For some reason I was near to sobbing. "And she has brought sunshine into my life too," I continued bitterly, "of all people, she seems to understand me best."

Silence followed this outburst. I couldn't bring myself to look at mother in case there were tears already in my eyes. But her eyes I knew were fixed on my face.

"We all understand you," Mother said at last, "But we do not want you to be unhappy . . ."

What empty words. I could not even reply. My happiness was in Eva's hand. They were denying me that hand for marriage thus plunging me into the depths of misery.

"Your father cares for your happiness more than you know," Mother went on, "Do not forget that . . . He looked so dark and troubled when you came in. It is bad for his health."

Something in her voice made me turn and look at her. Her hand was on the door knob and its movements were nervous I thought. But what struck me most was the urgent, pleading look that had come into her eyes. "Your father is a sick man," she said in a voice that chilled my heart, "I'll have to tell you this, now. You are not a child any more. Your father is very sick!"

"Sick!" I stammered. Our eyes held. Hers were wide and staring.

She leaned forward. Her voice was almost frightening as she said in a hoarse whisper. "Your father has got lung cancer. You are old enough to be told. . . You have heard him cough — So be careful what you do!"

She turned and left the room, leaving me stunned, not quite comprehending.

* * *

June passed away and with it most of the sunshine. Most of the time the weather was bleak and the sky dark and grey. And a dark shadow lay on our home. Sunshine seemed forever gone from my mother.

The grass was wet on a July afternoon as Eva and I sat on a block of stone near the school. She seemed excited as though she had something to tell me.

I also had lots to tell her. I felt for the ring to make sure it was still there.

She looked at me as if she could see through her dark glasses. She lay a little tender hand on my knee. "You look sad," she said.

How pretty she was! She had a smooth oval face, and a dimpled little cheek. I often wondered what colour her eyes would have been without the whiteness of her opaque cornea

"Sad?" I said with a smile, "but you can't see me!"

"Yes — but I can feel you are sad," she said, "What is wrong? Please tell me."

My voice was serious as I said, "Dad is worse .... We saw him again yesterday and I could —" I checked myself. "The doctor didn't look happy, I know Dad hasn't much of a chance."

Eva sat very still. I looked at her and felt happy. As always she understood... She turned away her face.

"How terrible!" she said.

How could I ever leave this angel? To me she was perfect — I wanted her as she was.

"Dad forgive me," I thought as I took out the ring, looked at it for a while thoughtfully. A wry smile came on my face. Wasn't life queer? Things turn out so very different from the way we picture them in our childish dreams.

A shiny diamond ring... The girl's shy eyes looking up at me as I slipped it on to her finger...

That had been my dream. I took her hand and slipped the cheap copper ring onto her finger. One or two imitation jewels gleamed. It didn't look too bad.

Her surprised face looked up.

"Wh — What is that?" she asked breathlessly.

"A ring," I said, "Don't you know. You and I are getting married." My voice was calm but there was a lump of excitement in my throat.

With her other hand she felt the ring. Suddenly she pulled it off and put it on my knee.

"No!" she said, "Let's wait a while!" Her voice was shaking and low, almost to a breathless whisper.

"Wait?" I asked, "What for?"

A slow smile lit up her face and she looked up to the sky. I had never seen her looking like this — happy and bright as an angel.

"Eva!" I said holding her hand to replace the ring, "I don't want to wait. I need you now. What do you want us to wait for?"

"Till I can see the ring," she said, "I want to see the ring!"

I stared at her. It was chilly but I felt sweat on my neck.

"What do you mean?" I asked.

I saw a tear creep down her cheek, underneath her dark glasses.

"That's what I wanted to tell you," she said, "I've got my bags packed!"

"Packed?" I didn't quite... See...

"Yes," she said, "I'm going to the hospital to receive a new cornea from — from someone else.... Someone who is about to—to cross over."

I stared at her. I licked my lips. "You mean that someone has —?"

She nodded, "I have no idea who it is," she said. "But God bless him. I don't know why he should want to do this for me. But I'm going to see again! God bless him...!

I just stared. I couldn't find any words to say. My heart was beating hard and loud — with unspeakable joy. But sorrow was equally great.

* * *

July too passed away and a great grey blanket seemed to have been lifted back to let the sun smile again. It was August, and life was once more brisk and lively.

I walked down the garden path whistling to myself. The oranges, for which I was aiming with my basket looked beautiful and yellow in the sun.

Suddenly I stopped, the smile dying on my face. I stood still. Then I walked towards the mound of earth a little way off.

I stood there looking at the grave. I swallowed hard. He was seeing me! I knew he was.

"I must say thanks," I said with a sudden burst of feeling. "You always had a kind heart and you really showed that with your last breath. Each time she looks at me with those lovely eyes..."

I broke off. How stupid to stand talking to a mute grave. It was like talking to oneself. There was no time to waste. on a fine morning like this — especially with Eva and mother back in the house waiting for the oranges.

eleven

father comes back

Little children are usually afraid of graves, but my father's grave down in our garden never seemed a fearful place for me in my childhood. It fascinated me, and very often I used to sit under the old Mugumo tree which grew close to the grave and cast a huge protective shadow over it. I used to sit there meditatively, and as the cool breeze shook the leaves off the tree and on to the silent, peaceful grave I thought of my father sleeping there under all that earth. Sleeping peacefully and eternally.

I thought of him not with any sadness or grief but with wonder and curiosity. I wondered about what my mother had told me — that my father would one day come out of the grave.

"One day," she used to say, "all the dead people will have life again. Then you will see your father for the first time." And sitting under the Mugumo tree I often expected to see the grave suddenly open up and my father crawl out. I wouldn't have been the least bit surprised or frightened if that had happened.

It was the only grave I knew and to my childish mind it was the only grave in the world. I was my mother's only child and I was often very lonely. There was no one to play with and consequently most of my time was spent musingly at the grave.

It was an attractive place — in a wild sort of way. Roses, ivy and other flowers grew in rich profusion and round the grave was a ring of stones. There was no gravestone.

My joining school at the age of six meant that I had less time to spend at the place. My world was now larger and my time was spent at three places: the house, the grave and the school. I liked school from the first and I never played truant. At least not until that cold day in July.

Two of my classmates, Jim and Tom, who were also the only good friends I had, persuaded me to hide from school that day so that we could steal mangoes from a farm some distance from the school. Not wishing to be called a coward I had outwardly readily, but inwardly apprehensively, agreed. I had never stolen before and I didn't like the plan. But my two friends, being more experienced than I was, had much influence over me and I always followed where they led (though I must add they had never led me along criminal paths before).

It wasn't as frightening as I had thought. Once safely up a mango tree all my anxiety ceased, and my friends and I attacked the delicious fruits with gusto. I even suggested that we revisit the orchard sometime.

But after my friends and I had parted and I had gone home a feeling of guilt slowly crept over me. I remembered what my mother had taught me and I was gripped by remorse. I was going into the garden to think quietly under the old by the graveside when my mother came out of the house and called to me.

"Dave," she called, "where are you off to?"

"Not far, mother," I said.

"Are you going to — to that tree?"

"I'm going into the garden," I answered.

"But it's so cold out there!"

"I know, I won't be long."

The grave was as peaceful as usual. I sat on the lee of the huge tree and watched the rustling leaves falling on to the fluttering flowers of the grave. And I wondered if *he* knew what I had done.

I felt rather tired and sleepy. We had walked far that day ...

How long I sat there I do not quite know but it must have been for several hours. Then suddenly the impossible happened. The grave seemed to split up and there was a wide deep crack in the middle. I watched spell bound, not daring to breathe. Fear possessed me. Then a head appeared, followed by shoulders. Nothing more. I stared at the face of a middle-aged man in a dark coat. The face was bearded and there was an ugly scar on its brow.

"My ... Father!" I exclaimed in a low voice.

He did not say a word. He did not even smile. He just looked at me with his sad eyes for a long time. Then he shook his head.

My eyes never left his face, and as I watched he slowly sank back into the grave. I screamed as the soil started covering him once more.

"Father!" I cried, "come back! Don't leave me, I beg you come back!"

"Dave! What's the matter?" a voice said. Suddenly I was being shaken.

"Dave!"

My eyes flickered open. I saw my mother bending over me anxiously.

"My father — he's gone!" I said, "He's gone back!"

"Your — father?" she whispered.

"He's gone back," I said still entranced, "into the grave."

I saw the tears well into her eyes. "Oh Dave," she said holding me to her breast, "You shouldn't come here so often, It isn't good for you." I looked up at her.

"Will he come again Mother?" I asked.

"He wasn't here, Dave," she said. "You have been dreaming child. Let's go home now."

We walked back to the house. It was not until we were back in the warm kitchen that my mother asked me to tell her about my dream. I told her.

"A man with a scar!" she interrupted.

I looked up quickly.

"Was my father like that, mother?" I asked her. She did not reply. She just held me close.

I did not go to my father's grave for days. I wanted to forget all about that dream. But I couldn't. I couldn't forget the way he had looked at me, and the fact that he had shaken his head at me and made me so sorrowful. Perhaps if he had smiled at me and tenderly spoken my name . . . But he hadn't. And I was to blame. Those mangoes . . . I felt miserable and a horrible feeling of guilt tortured me. Time brought no forgetfulness.

Then one day, a fortnight or so after my dream something happened and my feeling of guilt was brought to a sudden end. I had come home from school and been met by my mother at the door. She looked unusually excited and overjoyed. She grasped me and lifted me high, laughing joyously. I couldn't understand this. "Oh Davy boy!" She cried with tears of joy, "I've got a surprise!"

She set me down and pushed open the door. Inside the room, smiling at me from a chair was a lean man in a heavy black coat.

"Your father," my mother said.

My brain whirled. My mouth flew open. I felt faint.

"So this is my son," the lean man said coming towards me. He put an arm round my shoulder and we looked at each other. He was smiling. "He's a lot like me," he said.

My eyes left his face and I looked at mother. She was smiling through her tears. I felt mystified and dazed. I didn't know what to think. I was only sure of one thing: this man was not the man I had seen at the grave!

I looked at him again. He chuckled.

"I am sure you're puzzled," he said, "but take it from me you aren't seeing visions. I am your lost father." He turned to Mother. "Mary," he said, "let's not keep our son in the dark any longer. Let's tell him the long, long story!"

The door was closed behind us and we all sat down. The lean man was on my left and my mother was on my right. They told me the story. It wasn't a long story at all. I had been born, they said, when they were very poor. When I was still a tiny baby, my father had left us and gone to look for money. Through circumstances they didn't bother to explain, my parents had lost contact and my mother had thought he was dead. And when I grew up she told me so. But the grave I had always called my father's was really my grandfather's.

My mother concluded: "Now he has come back and will never leave us again." I saw the lean man squeeze her hand.

Even at that early age I could guess at the truth. My father had not left us to go and look for money. He had deserted us. Now he was back and had clearly been forgiven.

"Aren't you happy to see your father, Dave?" Mother asked me. I nodded and unconvincingly said I was. But the feeling inside me was not happiness. At that moment I was thinking of the man I had seen at the grave. I wished he was the one who had returned.

It is now fourteen years since all this happened but I still can see it vividly in my mind; the grave opening up, the head of my father — no, my grandfather — appearing from below; my anguished cry, "Don't leave!" still rings clearly in my head. I still can see the lean man smiling down at me and hear his words, "He looks a lot like me."

The Mugumo tree still stands today, faithfully and eternally watching over the grave. Sometimes I take the little path that leads from the house (not the old house but a larger one) and into the garden. I sit under the old tree watching the leaves fall on to the flowers below. And as they fall memories come flooding back.

I am sitting there now, and as I look up from my exercise book I see before me the scene as I have always known it. But it is not quite the same. Now there isn't one grave, there are two of them lying side by side. One is an old grave with an entangled mass of flowers growing over it. The other one has fewer flowers and is clearly more recently made. Who lie in them? Surely there ought to be some gravestones ....?

What for? Over my head carved in the bark of the huge tree are some words. They aren't very conspicuous and you might easily miss them. Still you don't have to peer very hard to read the words:

"HERE LIE MY PAPAS."

twelve

the spider's web

Inside the coffin, his body had become rigid. He tried to turn and only felt the prick of the nail. It had been hammered carelessly through the lid, just falling short of his shoulder. There was no pain but he felt irretrievable and alone, hemmed within the mean, stuffy box, knowing that outside was air. *As dust to dust* ... the pious preacher intoned out there, not without an edge of triumph. *This suicide, brethren . . .!* They had no right, these people had no right at all. They sang so mournfully over him, almost as if it would disappoint them to see him come back. But he would jump out yet, he would send the rusty nails flying back at them and teach that cheap-jack of an undertaker how to convert old trunks. He was not a third class citizen. *Let me out!* But he could not find the energy to cry out or even turn a little from the nail on his shoulder, as the people out there hastened to cash in another tune, for the padre might at any moment cry *Amen!* and commit the flesh deep into the belly of the earth whence it came. Somebody was weeping righteously between the pauses. He thought it was Mrs Njogu. Then in the dead silence that followed he was being posted into the hole and he felt himself burning up already as his mean little trunk creaked at the joints and nudged its darkness in on him like a load of sins. *Careful, careful, he is not a heap of rubbish ...* That was Mr. Njogu. Down, slowly down, the careless rope issued in snappy mean measures like a spider's web and knocked his little trunk against the sides to warn the loud gates that he was coming to whoever would receive him. It caved in slowly, the earth, he could feel, and for the first time he felt important. He seemed to matter now, as all eyes no doubt narrowed into the dark hole at this moment, with everybody hissing *poor soul; gently, gently.* Then *snap!* The rope gave way — one portion of the dangling thing preferring to recoil into the tight-fisted hands out there — and he felt shot towards the bottom head downwards, exploding into the gates of hell with a loud, unceremonious *Bang!*

Ngotho woke up with a jump. He mopped the sweat on the tail of his sheet. This kind of thing would bring him no good. Before, he had been dreaming of beer parties or women or fights with bees as he tried to smoke them out for honey. Now, lately, it seemed that when he wasn't being smoked out of this city where he so very much belonged and yet never belonged, he was either pleading his case at the White Gates or being condemned to hell in cheap coffins. *This kind of thing just isn't healthy ...*

But he was in top form. He flung the blanket away. He bent his arms at the elbow for exercise. He shot them up and held them there like a surrender. *No that will not do.* He bent them again and pressed his fingers on his shoulders. They gathered strength, knitting into a ball so that his knuckles sharpened. Then he shot a dangerous fist to the left and held it there, tightly, not yielding a step, until he felt all stiff and blood pumped at his forehead. Dizziness overpowered him and his hand fell dead on the bed. Then a spasm uncoiled his right which came heavily on the wall and, pained, cowered. Was he still a stranger to the small dimensions of his only room even after eight years?

But it wasn't the first time anyhow. So, undaunted, he sprang twice on the bed for more exercise. Avoiding the spring that had fetched his thigh yesterday morning between the bulges in the old mattress, he hummed ***Africa nchi yetu*** and shot his leg down the bed. Swa — ah! That would be three shillings for another sheet through the back doors of the Khoja Mosque. Ngotho dragged himself out of bed.

It was a beautiful Sunday morning. He felt he had nothing to worry about so long as he did not make the mistake of going to church. Churches depressed him. But that dream still bothered him. At least they could have used a less precipitate rope. And those nails, didn't he have enough things pricking him since Mrs. Knight gave him a five-pound handshake saying Meet you in England and Mrs Njogu came buzzing in as his new memsahib borrowing two shillings from him?

Ngotho folded his arms at his chest and yawned. He took his moustache thoughtfully between his fingers and curled it sharp like a bull's horns. At least she could have returned it. It was not as if the cost of living had risen the way people borrowed from you these days. He stood at the door of the two-room house which he shared with the other servant who, unlike him, didn't cook for memsahib. Instead, Kago went on errands, trimmed the grass and swept the compound, taking care to trace well the dog's mess for the night. Already Ngotho could see the early riser as good as sniffing and scanning the compound after the erratic manner of Wambui last night. (Wambui was the brown Alsatian dragged from the village and surprised into civilisation, a dog-collar and tinned bones by Mrs. Njogu. Her friend Elsie Bloom, a widow, also kept one and they took their bitches for a walk together.) Ngotho cleared his throat.

"Hei, Kago!"

Kago, who was getting frost-bite, rubbed his thumb between his toes and turned round.

"How is the dog's breakfast?"

"Nyukwa!"

Ngotho laughed.

"You don't have to insult my mother," he said. "Tinned bones for Wambui and corn flakes for memsahib are the same thing. We both hang if we don't get them."

Kago leant on his broom, scratched the top of his head dull-wittedly, and at last saw that Ngotho had a point there.

He was a good soul, Kago was, and subservient as a child. There was no doubt about his ready aggressiveness where men of his class were concerned it was true, but when it came to Mrs. Njogu he wound tail between his legs and stammered. This morning he was feeling at peace with the world.

"Perhaps you are right," he said to Ngotho. Then diving his thumb between his toes he asked if there was a small thing going on that afternoon — like a beer party.

"The Queen!"

At the mention of the name, Kago forgot everything about drinking, swerved round and felt a thousand confused things beat into his head simultaneously. Should he go on sweeping and sniffing or should he get the Bob's Tinned? Should he un-tin the Bob's Tinned or should he run for the Sunday paper? Mrs. Njogu, alias queen, wasn't she more likely to want Wambui brushed behind the ear? Or was she now coming to ask him why the rope lay at the door while Wambui ran about untied?

With his bottom towards memsahib's door, Kago assumed a busy pose and peeped between his legs. But memsahib wasn't bothered about him, at least not yet. She stood at the door legs askew and admonished Ngotho about the corn flakes.

Kago breathed a sigh of relief and took a wild sweep at the broom. He saw Ngotho back against the wall of their servants'-quarter and suppressed a laugh. After taking a torrent of English words, Ngotho seemed to tread carefully the fifty violent paces between the two doors, the irreconcilable gap between the classes. As he approached Mrs. Njogu, he seemed to sweep a tactful curve off the path, as if to move up to the wall first and then try to back in slowly towards the Master's door and hope memsahib would make way. For her part, the queen flapped her wings and spread herself luxuriously, as good as saying You will have to kneel and dive in through my legs. Then she stuck out her tongue twice, heaved her breasts, spat milk and honey onto the path, and disappeared into the hive. Ngotho followed her.

Kago scratched his big toe and sat down to laugh.

* * *

Breakfast for memsahib was over. Ngotho came out of the house to cut out the painful corn in his toe with the kitchen knife. He could take the risk and it pleased him. But he had to move to the other end of the wall. Mr. Njogu was flushing the toilet and he might chance to open the small opaque window and see the otherwise clean kitchen knife glittering in the sun on dirty toe nails.

Breakfast. Couldn't memsahib trust him with the sugar or milk even after four years? Must she buzz around him as he measured breakfast-for-two? He had nothing against corn flakes. In fact ever since she became suspicious, he had found himself eating more of her meals whenever she was not in sight, taking also some sugar in his breast pocket. But he had come to hate himself for it and felt it was a coward's way out. Still, what was he to do? Mrs. Njogu had become more and more of a stranger and he had even caught himself looking at her from an angle where formerly he had stared her straight in the face. He had wanted to talk to her, to assure her that he was still her trusted servant, but everything had become more entangled and sensitive. She would only say he was criticising, and if he wasn't happy what was he waiting for? But if he left, where was he to go? Unemployment had turned loose upon the country as it had never done before. Housewives around would receive the news of his impertinence blown high and wide over Mrs. Njogu's telephone before he approached them for a job, and set their dogs on him.

Ngotho scratched at his grey hair and knew that respect for age had completely deserted his people. Was this the girl he once knew as Lois back in his home village? She had even been friends with his own daughter. A shy, young thing with pimples and thin legs, she taught at the village school and had been everybody's good example. She preferred to wear cheap skirts than see her aging parents starve for lack of money.

"Be like Lois," mothers warned their daughters and even spanked them to press the point. What they meant in fact was that their daughters should, like Lois, stay unmarried longer and not simply run off with some young man in a neat tie who refused to pay the dowry. Matters became worse for such girls when suddenly Lois became heroine of the village. She went to jail.

*   *   *

It was a General Knowledge class. Lois put the problem word squarely on the blackboard. The lady supervisor who went round the schools stood squarely at the other end, looking down the class. Lois swung her stick up and down the class and said,

"What is the Commonwealth, children? Don't be shy, what does this word mean?"

The girls chewed their thumbs.

"Come on!" she shouted and seeing it was hopeless said, "All right. We shall start from the *beginning*. Who rules England?"

Slowly, the girls turned their heads round and faced the white supervisor. Elizabeth, they knew they should say. But how could Lois bring them to this? England sounded venerable enough. Must they go further now and let the white lady there at the back hear the Queen of England mispronounced, or even uttered by such tender things with the smell of last night's onions in their breath? Who would be the first? They knit their knuckles under the desks, looked into their exercise books, and one by one said they didn't know. One or two brave ones threw their heads back again, met with a strange look in the white queen's eye which spelt disaster, immediately swung their eyes onto the blackboard and catching sight of Lois's stick, began to cry.

"It is as if you have never heard of it." Lois was losing patience. "All right, I'll give you another start. Last start. What is this country?"

Simultaneously, a flash of hands shot up from under the desks and thirty four breaths of maize and onions clamoured,

"A colony!"

Slowly, the lady supervisor measured out light taps down the classroom and having eliminated the gap that came between master and servant, stood face to face with Lois.

The children chewed at their rubbers.

Then the white queen slapped Lois across the mouth and started for the door. But Lois caught her by the hair, slapped her back once, twice, and spat into her face. Then she gave her a football kick and swept her out with a right.

When at last Lois looked back into the class, she only saw torn exercise books flung on the floor. Thirty-four pairs of legs had fled home through the window, partly to be protected from the white queen's government which was certain to come, and partly to spread the formidable news of their new queen and heroine.

* * *

Queen she certainly was, Ngotho thought as he sat by the wall and backed against it. Corn flakes in bed; expensive skirts; cigarettes. Was this she? Mr. Njogu had come straight from the University College in time to secure a shining job occupied for years by a *mzungu*. Then a neat car was seen to park by Lois's house. In due course these visits became more frequent and alarming but no villager was surprised when eventually Njogu succeeded in dragging Lois away from decent society. He said paying the dowry was for people in the mountains.

As luck would have it for Ngotho, Mr. and Mrs. Knight left and Mr. and Mrs. Njogu came to occupy the house. He was glad to cook and wash a black man's towels for a change. And, for a short time at any rate, he was indeed happy. Everybody had sworn that they were going to build something together, something challenging and responsible, something that would make a black man respectable in his own country. He had been willing to serve, to keep up the fire that had eventually smoked out the white man. From now on there would be no more revenge, and no more exploitation. Beyond this, he didn't expect much for himself; he knew that there would always be masters and servants.

Ngotho scratched himself between the legs and sunk against the wall. He stared at the spider that slowly built its web meticulously under the verandah roof. He threw a light stone at it. He only alerted the spider.

Had his heart not throbbed with thousands of others that day as each time he closed his eyes he saw a vision of something exciting, a legacy of responsibilities that demanded a warrior's spirit? Had he not prayed for oneness deep from the heart? But it seemed to him now that a common goal had been lost sight of and he lamented it. He could not help but feel that the warriors had laid down their arrows and had parted different ways to fend for themselves. And as he thought of their households, he saw only the image of Lois who he dared call nothing but memsahib now. She swam big and muscular in his mind.

Ngotho wondered whether this was the compound he used to know. Was this path connecting master and servant the one that had been so straight during Mrs. Knight's reign?

Certainly he would never want her back. He had been kicked several times by Mr. Knight and had felt what it was like to be hit with a frying pan by Mrs. Knight as she reminded him to be grateful. But it had all been so direct, no ceremonies: they didn't like his broad nose. They said so. They thought there were rats under his bed. There were. They teased that he hated everything white and yet his hair was going white on his head like snow, a cool white protector while below the black animal simmered and plotted: wouldn't he want it cut? No, he wouldn't. Occasionally, they would be impressed by a well-turned turkey or chicken and say so over talk of the white man's responsibility in Africa. If they were not in the mood they just dismissed him and told him not to forget the coffee. Ngotho knew that all this was because they were becoming uneasy and frightened, and that perhaps they had to point the gun at all black men now at a time when even the church had taken sides. But whatever the situation in the house, there was nevertheless a frankness about the black-and-white relationship where no ceremonies or apologies were necessary in a world of mutual distrust and hate. And if Mrs. Knight scolded him all over the house, it was Mr. Knight who eventually seemed to lock the bedroom door and come heavily on top of her and everybody else although, Ngotho thought, they were all ruled by a woman in England.

Ngotho walked heavily to the young tree planted three years ago by Mrs. Njogu and wondered why he should have swept a curve off the path that morning, as memsahib filled the door. He knew it wasn't the first time he had done that. Everything had become crooked, subtle, and he had to watch his step. His monthly vernacular paper said so. He felt cornered. He gripped the young tree by the scruff of the neck and shook it furiously. What the hell was wrong with some men anyway? Had Mr. Njogu become a male weakling in a fat queen bee's hive, slowly being milked dry and sapless, dying? Where was the old warrior who at the end of the battle would go home to his wife and make her moan under his heavy sweat? All he could see now as he shook the tree was a line of neat houses. There the warriors had come to their battle's end and parted, to forget other warriors and to be mothered to sleep without even knowing it, meeting only occasionally to drink beer and sing traditional songs. And where previously the spear lay by the bed-post, Ngotho now only saw a conspiracy of round tablets while a *Handbook of novel Techniques* lay by the pillow.

He had tried to understand. But as he looked at their pregnant wives he could foresee nothing but a new generation of innocent snobs who would be chauffeured off to school in neat caps hooded over their eyes so as to obstruct vision. There they would learn that the other side of the city was dirty. Ngotho spat right under the tree. Once or twice he would have liked to kick Mr. Njogu. He looked all so sensibly handsome and clean as he buzzed after his wife on a broken wing and — a spot of jam on his tie — said he wanted the key to the car.

He had also become very sensitive and self-conscious. Ngotho couldn't complain a little or even make a joke about the taxes without somebody detecting a subtler intention behind that smile, where the servant was supposed to be involved in full-scale plotting. And there was behind the master and the queen now a bigger design, a kind of pattern meticulously fenced above the hive; a subtle web, at the centre of which lurked the spider which protected, watched and jailed. Ngotho knew only too well that the web had been slowly, quietly spun, and a pebble thrown at it would at best alert and fall back impotent on the ground.

He took a look at the other end of the compound. Kago had fallen asleep, while Wambui ran about untied, the rope still lying at the door; in a noose. Kago wore an indifferent grin. Ngotho felt overpowered, trapped, alone. Someday, one could be driven to suicide. He spat in Kago's direction and plucked a twig off one of the branches on the tree. The tree began to bleed. He tightened his grip and shed the reluctant leaves down. Just what had gone wrong with the gods?

The old one had faithfully done his job when that fig tree near Ngotho's village withered away as predicted by the tribal seer. It had been the local news and lately, it was rumoured, some business man would honour the old god by erecting a hotel on the spot. Ngotho hardly believed in any god at all. The one lived in corrupted blood, the other in corruption itself. But at least while they kept neat themselves they could have honoured the old in a cleaner way. How could this new saviour part the warriors different ways into isolated compartments, to flush their uneasy hotel toilets all over the old one?

Ngotho passed a reverent hand over his wrinkled forehead and up his white hair. He plucked another twig off the dangerous tree. Something was droning above his ear.

"What are you doing to my tree?"

The buzzing had turned into a scream.

"I — I want to pick my teeth." Ngotho unwrapped a row of defiant molars.

The queen flapped her wings and landed squarely on the ground. Then she was heaving heavily, staring at him out of small eyes. He tried to back away from her eyes. Beyond her, in the background, he caught sight of Mr. Njogu through the bedroom window polishing his spectacles on his pyjama sleeve, trying desperately to focus — clearly — on the situation outside. A flap of the wing and Ngotho felt hit right across the mouth, by the hand that had once hit the white lady. Then the queen wabbled in midflight, settled at the door, and screamed at Mr. Njogu to come out and prove he was a man.

Mr. Njogu didn't like what he saw. He threw his glasses away and preferred to see things blurred.

"These women," he muttered, and waved them away with a neat pyjama sleeve. Then he buried his head under the blanket and snored. It was ten o'clock.

Ngotho stood paralysed. He had never been hit by a woman before, since he left his mother's hut. Involuntarily, he felt his eyes snap shut and his eyelids burn red, violently in the sun. Then out of the spider's web in his mind, policemen, magistrates and third class undertakers flew in profusion. He opened up, sweating, and the kitchen knife in his hand fell down, stabbing the base of the tree where it vibrated once, twice and fell flat on its side, dead.

Then with a cry, he grabbed it and rushed into the house. But Mr. Njogu saw him coming as the knife glittered nearer and clearer in his direction, and leapt out of bed.

Suddenly the horror of what he had done caught Ngotho. He could hear the queen crying hysterically into the telephone, while Mr. Njogu locked himself in the toilet. Ngotho looked at the kitchen knife in his hand. He had only succeded in stabbing Mr. Njogu in the thigh and the knife had now turned red on himself. Soon the sticky web would stretch a thread. And he would be caught as he never thought he would when first he felt glad to work for Lois.

thirteen

something in common

Samuel Ngure tried to stand up, saw the ends of the counter swing pendulum up and down and, staggering, knew that he was in trouble with his wife. He was getting drunk at three o'clock in the afternoon. And if that wasn't enough trouble with Mrs. Esther Wanjiru Ngure, then he wasn't Mr. Samuel Ngure. But perhaps she might understand. It was three weeks before the elections and customers were fighting at the top of their drunken voices about the two candidates. He couldn't help staying. But staying meant getting drunk. He told himself it had to be positively one last one for the road.

It was a dusty road as he made for it at last three hours later with good news for Wanjiru. That would save him tonight, the good news. But he hadn't far to go before he was surprised to see one of the candidates. The latter wore a beaded cap and exuberantly waved a flywhisk. If he hadn't stopped him, Samuel Ngure might not have recognised him. In the five years he had been in parliament Mangau had caught on the popular political fashion in dress and had ventured a goatee.

As the tie was for the capitalists, James Mangau, Esq., M.P. for Mangari East, had long discarded it as decadent, in favour of a patriotic multi-coloured T-shirt which supposedly identified him with Ngure.

Ngure was a shoemaker by profession. For several years, he had hammered the nail into the shoes of the capitalists seven days a week before his fellow shoemakers elected him President of their union.

The M.P. approached him and Ngure knew that he was set on taking his vote away from him for a further five years. He, in turn, was bent upon sweeping him as wide a berth as possible. He would decline even to talk to him. But the M.P. called out 'Sir!' four times and Samuel Ngure, Esq., felt a little flattered.

"Haven't we met before?" Mangau asked.

Ngure said yes, they had met before. But he had not seen him since he took away his vote five years ago.

Mangau assured him that the vote had been in the good hands of the party. Like the Lord's good talents, it had been fully utilised. Just in the way of a small illustration, he had for instance been busy fighting the battle in parliament about that road, and also about piped water.

Ngure looked up the road. Even in his drunken state, he could see it couldn't be more dusty. He said so.

Mangau skipped the issue. Quickly, he asked Ngure if he hadn't heard his famous speech about the Chinese. He had branded them as communists.

Ngure replied that as far as he knew, the Chinese had always been communists and were happy about it. In any event, Mangau must underestimate the shoemakers if he thought they would vote him into parliament just to have a lot of talk about the Chinese.

"How about that piped water?"

Mangau was in no mood for that one either. "These days," he said, "no country is an island. You simply must look broader into the world, Chinesewise and otherwise, don't you know?"

"You do look a little broader yourself since we saw you last."

Mangau, who was a little drunk, told Ngure to say that again.

"You also promised my union that —"

Mangau cut him short. He said that Ngure should have heard what Confucius said on State in regard to other states. Quite simply, people must learn to be a bit broad-minded.

Ngure fired back. Confusion or Confucius, he wasn't interested. He would be more impressed if people kept their election pledges. Was that what they had voted for him to learn? "I should have thought that through you the government would learn our problems."

But there was no stopping Mangau. It seemed that Confucius was a wise Chinaman who said many good things. If he was alive today the Chinese would vote him Prime Minister for life. His wisdom was enough to send fifty aspirants safely to parliament.

"If that is so", Ngure said angrily, "it is a direct contradiction of what you have just said about the Chinese. I understand, however, that that *is* politics."

At this interjection, the M.P. for Mangari East hastily added that for all he cared, Confucius might please himself. "My one interest at heart has always been your interests, my constituents' interests."

"You weren't doing us much service the way you almost crossed to the Government benches three years ago."

"Oh, that? It was a slip of the bench. Good sense did after all prevail, didn't it? You know, I believe the difference between you and me is purely academic. It is one of terms Remove the semantics and what have *we* got? One heart to the problems, one language. Between you and me we have a lot in common. Tell the Shoemakers' and Allied Workers' Union to vote for me."

"Between you and me," Ngure said, "I can see nothing but too many miles of dust and promises." He walked away.

No sooner had Ngure disappeared out of Mangau's sight than he was approached by the latter's opponent.

"I have been watching you from that shop", Njoroge began, "being molested by that Democratic Party thug. You quite showed him that your father's clan isn't made of women".

Ngure told the young man that he couldn't spare the time. He had already heard it all before.

"That Democrat must have been talking off his beaded cap," said the young man, undeterred.

Ngure looked the lanky young fellow up and down. With luck, he might be sent to parliament and put some meat on those bones.

"Young man," he said, "ambition was never made of weaker stuff. What do you want to break your neck in this race for?"

"I want to go to parliament —"

"Most impressive," said Ngure. "When? You don't look more than twenty-three to me. I have no intention of voting any more youth wingers into that House."

"Care for a drink?" the young man offered. "We could talk in there."

Ngure looked at his watch. Then at the generous young man. Then he cast his eyes towards the sinking sun. And then — he thought of Esther Wanjiru. She would have to wait. But at least tonight was the one night she wasn't going to talk him out of his own house. He agreed that it was still very much on the early side yet. He would have that drink, if Njoroge pleased.

"Look at me," said Njoroge as he fingered his glass in a private room at the corner of the Wananchi Bar. "Young blood. Young blood is what I've got. New ideas —."

"That's too fast, that's too fast," said Ngure. "Did I understand you to say 'new ideas'?"

"Yes, what's more —"

Ngure rose up. He took the young man by the scruff of the neck. Then, calmly, he led him to the open window.

"Look over there," he said, "what do you see?"

Njoroge said he could see nothing but trees and the dusty road. The dust did look somewhat aesthetically golden in the evening sun.

Ngure suggested they stopped getting carried away. "Five years ago," he said, "Mangau came to me. He told me that if I called the S.A.W.U. to vote for him, he would see that it was all tarmac. I'm not interested in new ideas. I want someone to carry that old one out!"

As Njoroge disengaged himself from the latter's grip, he promised to press the government to tarmac that most important road in the heart of their farming constituency. What is more, he would see that there was no more dowry price. What is more he would ban the mini-skirt. What is more he would stop magazines publishing stories written about Africans by English housewives. After that he warmed up to the theme of old heads on young shoulders. In politics, he pointed out, new wine more than stands the test against the old. This could be exemplified by the fact that unlike some old loony who had just been soliciting Ngure's vote, he was at least literate enough to tell a copy of Hansard when he saw one. He gave the President of the S.A.W.U. the party bull-sign with his right thumb.

"Stop bull-dozing me!" Ngure shouted. "Can you defend yourselves against some grievous charges made by your opponent. He says you are all communists."

The young man was more than ready. The root of the trouble was, he said, not Mr. Mao Tse-Tung's thoughts but Uncle Sam. Even as they talked, Njoroge confided, there were over two thousand Mexican Joes all over the country who passed as peace corps and tourists but any shoemaker worth his tool —

"Hey?"

— any peace-loving citizen could tell they were CIA's and spies. You could recognise them by their binoculars, cameras, big-frame sunglasses, cowboy hats, and the Hand-of-friendship that they were more than willing to extend...

Ngure lost his patience. No shoemaker who had hammered away at the cow's hide for years would support an able-bodied young oaf in parliament just to have a lot of talk about some tourists.

"If you vote for me," said Njoroge drinking to his own health, "they will go. What is more the demands of the S.A.W.U. about better working conditions will be met. I will also speak out in no uncertain terms that the proposed legislation against more than one wife is detrimentally opposed to

African Socialism, especially considering that the latest census shows there would be many old maids to pay. Vote for Njoroge," he said, "and you can all marry ten wives if you wish."

"Ten wives, my goats!" Ngure shouted. "Get out of here. Who wants ten wives in a country where you can't even beat the one wife you've got in peace without some Blackenglishman of a magistrate giving you a silly little pointer about 'decent conduct in decent society'? You fellows have got something in common and I don't like it."

"Well, it's either Mangau or me, and I trust you. Please vote for me. After all, there is no Independent candidate. And abstention is negation, remember."

"Who says there is no Independent candidate? I must say your eloquence is overwhelming. The shoemakers have just decided to back one."

"What!"

"*What is more,* you are going to have the first woman in parliament."

"What!!'

"Wanjiru. Tough and honest Esther Wanjiru, President of the Market Women Agitators' League. She will be more than willing to turn you fellows inside out at that political rally tomorrow. And," Ngure added, "I shouldn't be there when she begins talking."

"Well, I will be," said Njoroge, courageously.

Ngure took his half-full glass. With one eye closed, he saw the distorted face of the brave young man through the top half. Then, furiously, he threw his head backwards and downed the contents.

"Distorted!" He banged the glass on the table.

He stood up. He wiped the froth off his lips.

"Than-hic thanks for the drink," he said. "I'll pay for it."

"Trouble is," he hiccupped to himself as he swept his way towards the counter, "she might turn parliament inside out talking about the emancipation of her sex. You just can't trust anybody these days."

"No," said the young man, his head in his hands, "you just can't trust anybody these or any other days."

fourteen

the wind

Mumbi hesitated at the door, nervously chewing a finger nail. She was fifteen minutes late and she felt that it would be very unwise to enter the office without some lie. For in this case the truth would only be sniffed at and thrown back in her face as a lie. A good lie might be accepted as the truth. The truth was that her bus had failed to turn up. In her rather remote part of the reserve there was only one bus that could get her to town in good time. There she would have ample time to wait for another bus that took her across the town into the Industrial area. But today her precious bus had failed to turn up at the usual time. The little familiar crowd that had waited with increasing agitation at the bus stop with her had been as baffled as she had been. Fortunately she had been offered a lift by a kind gentleman — a business man she knew — but then she was already far behind time.

With a vague half-constructed lie that she hoped would smoothen itself out as she told it to Mr. Singh, Mumbi opened the door and cautiously peeped in.

Mr. Singh merely glanced up from his work and then he seemed to decide that the door had been moved by a particularly strong breeze. He turned back to his work. A large heavy man, Tarlok Singh s/o Gian Singh Panesar gave the impression of having been poured into his seat. With his coloured turban, he reminded one, when he sat up, of a forbidding mountain that had crimson snow upon its summit. His face, like that of a mountain, seemed incapable of registering any emotion and rarely did. Thus any feelings he might have felt somewhere in the depths of his interior on seeing the latecomer were unreflected on his countenance.

Mumbi hesitated at the doorway with a mixture of surprise, disappointment and relief. These feelings in a curious reaction seemed to explode into a flush of anger. She had her own interpretation of Mr. Singh's casual glance.

"Who else?" his eyes, beady through the thick lenses, had seemed to say, "Who else could come in fifteen minutes late but our Miss Mumbi? And what else could be expected of her?" He had not given her a chance to explain — or rather to tell her lie. And yet as she remembered Friday evening when she had sneaked away early behind his back (and a few other occasions when she had been naughty) a feeling of remorse smote her. She must be good, she resolved. Never again would she annoy Mr. Singh.

Mumbi looked across the large office at her friend Susan. Susan was looking her way and her face broke into one of her breezy smiles. Mumbi's dark moment was instantly gone. She smiled back, closed the door and walked across to Susan. The two girls loved each other and nothing could part them. They worked side by side and often laughed so much that Mr. Singh had threatened to transfer one of them to some other department. Susan was curious as to why her friend was so late. Mumbi told her.

"I keep on telling you to quit home and stay here in town," Susan triumphantly said, "You would never have any trouble with the buses."

They had been through all that before and Mumbi did not want to be dragged into it again. As she had many times told Susan, it was not that she was against staying in town but her parents would never allow her to. They were an ageing couple, deeply religious and with a fervent hatred of the city and all the evils simple country folk like them usually associated with it. It had unmanned their children, breaking down their morals and beliefs. Indeed Sodom and Gomorrha seemed to have been reincarnated in these modern times in a new form as abominable as that which the Almighty hand had, in the days of old, wiped out from the face of the earth.

"You must really press them to let you come!" said Susan, "Gosh! Think of the rainy days when your dress is such a sight and your shoes are leaden with mud. And think of your report. Coming as late as this doesn't help at all. That old cow may appear dumb but he's not all that stupid, I assure you!.

Mumbi looked at her quickly.

"You think he — Mr. Singh wouldn't do that!"

Susan shrugged. "How do you know?" she said, "Anyhow if you want to get out of this and be a secretary you'd better be on good terms with him."

Mumbi's face was for a moment shadowed with a worried frown. "I don't think he dislikes me too much yet." She looked at Susan inquiringly for an opinion.

"I wouldn't know," her friend replied with a sigh, "The man is dumb. You never know what is going on in his head.

Just like you, for almost two years I thought he liked me. That made me work like hell — and where has it led me?"

Mumbi sympathised with Susan. She yearned for promotion. She had been a little more than three years in the Company and was bitter at having been "pinned down" all the time. She wanted a better grade and her ambition was to be a Secretary at the Company's headquarters in the city. Sometimes girls were recruited for these posts from the Industrial area branch but her hopes were always dashed. Somehow she was always passed over. Naturally her bitterness was mainly for the boss in the sales office, Mr. Tarlok Singh.

"There is a rumour that he is going back to India. All of them seem to be going back. I'm sure we'll have a chance now!"

Mumbi gave a long searching look at the face of Mr. Singh. At the same moment Mr. Singh looked up and their eyes met.

When he spoke, Mr. Singh had a quiet, rumbling voice. His lips hardly moved and his voice seemed to come from a hollow chamber within his solid body.

"If I were you, Miss Mumbi," he said, "I would start my work now. Your tray, I observe, is full."

For the first time Mumbi saw her tray, too, and let out a muffled cry of dismay at the heaped, disorderly pile of letters, statements and invoices.

"You have yourself to blame," whispered Susan laughing at her. "You should have worked over-time with the rest of us last Friday."

"And missed my last bus . ." Mumbi wailed inserting a sheet of paper hurriedly in the typewriter.

"Why don't you come to your senses and settle —"

"Oh shut up — Mr. Singh is watching us."

But it was not Mr. Singh that Mumbi was worried about. The man who was making her nervous at that moment was one of the clerks, Mbogo. He was looking at her very darkly and a warning signal flared in her mind.

Mbogo was one of the senior clerks and somehow always seemed to be the busiest in the room. Naturally the two girls had plenty of things to type for him. A fastidious, ill-tempered man, he was generally unpopular in the sales office, especially among the Indian clerks of his grade.

His eye continued to bore holes on Mumbi's face for a while. Frantically she wondered how she was supposed to type correctly if eyes like those...

"Mumbi!"

Mbogo had a sharp voice that made heads jerk up all around as though a piece of metal had clattered to the floor.

Both girls had stopped typing and Mumbi couldn't get rid of a tense feeling in her breast. If only Mbogo would learn to call people more quietly.

"Don't go. He should come to you." Susan said.

"Come here, Mumbi."

But Mumbi didn't want to attract further attention. Already Mr. Singh had been roused to curiosity.

"No, let me hear what he wants to say," she said and bravely walked to Mbogo's desk.

"Mumbi," Mbogo said looking up from a letter he held in his hands, "I have just been looking at a specimen of your typing, which is a letter supposed to advise a distinguished customer of ours about an important business transaction. Have a look at it and compare it with the original draft I had given you, and tell me what is wrong with it."

While he was speaking she had already noticed a spelling mistake. She regretted her over-hurried typing last Friday evening. She took the draft and looked at it unseeingly.

"Compare it with my draft." Mbogo said.

"There was so much to do. We were in such a hurry —"

"That is no excuse. What is the use of sending a letter to these people if we can't even spell their name? Were you quite awake when you typed that letter?"

"I told you. We were so busy!" Mumbi flashed out.

Behind her Mr. Singh had sat up. As the supervisor in the sales office he always liked being in the know about little matters that came up. Unable to contain his curiosity he leaned forward.

"What is it, Mr. Mbogo?" he asked in his quiet voice, "show, me."

Mbogo rose, shaking his head aggrievedly.

"Mistakes," he said, "Figures wrong. And even the name of the Company to whom my letter is addressed she wrongly spelt. Have a look."

Quietly Mr. Singh examined the letter. Finally he called Mumbi to his desk. His face looked grave.

"You have been careless in the typing of this letter, Miss Mumbi," Mr. Singh said, "Tell me, how you make all these mistakes?"

Mumbi faltered, "I — I was in a hurry. There was so much to do last Friday evening and I —"

"But I seem to remember that Friday you left early. Without my permission, no?"

His eyes searched her face and she dropped hers in shame. Then she looked up.

"I had to catch my last bus," she said contritely.

She tried to read the look in his eyes but whatever was written in them was in a language meaningless to her. In a solemn voice Mr. Singh told her to retype the letter correctly and hand it back to Mr. Mbogo. She walked unseeingly back to her desk with a heavy heart. She recalled Susan's words: "The old cow may appear dumb but he's not all that stupid, I assure you!"

"The beast. The nasty beast!" Susan said furiously as Mumbi sat down. "The chap acts like he was our supervisor or something."

Mumbi smiled wearily, "Mbogo?" she said and shrugged.

"It's vain ambition!" declared Susan, "He is the careful, responsible clerk whose keen eye never misses a thing. He only wants to attract Mr. Singh's attention."

Mumbi sighed, "And be promoted?" she said. "Isn't that the whole game? Everybody is talking about the wind of change. Who isn't hoping it will blow his way?"

"But undermining others . . .!" protested Susan.

"He was quite justified," Mumbi pointed out. "I made a perfect mess of his letter. I'm hopeless sometimes." She added sadly.

"Yes," said Susan, "when you rise in support of chaps like Mbogo."

* * *

Susan's flat was in the African suburb of Maringo. Some men from Maringo who also worked in the Industrial Area branch often walked the distance. But to her this was an extreme and uncalled-for measure of economy and she always took a bus.

She had always wanted Mumbi to stay with her, but her wish was not realised until her room-mate —who was also called Susan — got married and moved out. In distress Susan pleaded to her friend for the umpteenth time to move in...

"I feel so lost and lonely. I can't stay all alone. The rent in any case is too high for me to face all by myself. Girlie, how can you torture me this way?"

Mumbi had no choice but to move in. She had always wanted to, and Susan's new problems gave her the excuse she needed in a final showdown with her parents. She had once spent a night at Susan's flat, a modest place, rather cramped and hot. She had thought of their grim, wattle-and-daub house that was always smoky and dimly-lit, and a wistful look had come into her eyes that night. She would look for a chance to get away from the reserve to the exciting city. Her chance had now come. She could leave without any guilt conscience. Her friend was in trouble and she had to immigrate into the city to her rescue.

Her parents were sad and afraid. But they had seen it coming. All the young people wanted the city. They were mad about it. This Sodom-Gomorrah had ensnared so many young people they had watched grow around them. It had been wishful thinking to hope their own would be spared. She packed and resignedly they bade her farewell.

Her departure coincided with Mr. Singh's resignation from the Company. In the same week-end that she left home there was a party in the Sales Office to bid Mr. Singh farewell. There was music and drinks and the general atmosphere was relaxed. But it was Mumbi's first party of the kind and she felt out of place and lonely. She did not know how to dance and was afraid to try any strong drink. Susan, who was having a good time, was understanding and from time to time escaped from other company to dispel her loneliness.

"Have some sherry," she advised.

"Some what? No — I don't think I should..."

"Do you some good," she insisted and poured out a glass for Mumbi. Mumbi sipped a little and couldn't make up her mind whether she liked it. Susan grinned and nodded. Then she disappeared into the crowd again. A moment later Mumbi saw her dancing in Mbogo's arms and was very surprised. Afterwards Susan came to her again looking flushed and happy. The drinks were beginning to work on her.

"This is great, girlie," she said laughing, "I've just danced with our next boss."

Mumbi stared, "You don't say! Mbogo...?"

"Why not? He could easily be. Let's humour him anyway and make him forget past differences."

"He couldn't possibly be our next boss!" Mumbi said in alarm.

"Well," Susan replied, "The position as far as I know is vacant. If you ask me Mbogo is the best man for the job, all prejudice apart!"

She gulped down some whisky and made a grimace.

"It's tough," she said. "It's tough, I know."

She sighed and got up. The next minute she was swallowed again into the crowd.

Mumbi was happy when the party was over, late in the evening. At once the problem of transport loomed large in her mind but Susan had already seen to that. She led Mumbi outside where the moonlight was bright and beautiful to where the cars were parked. In one of the cars (she didn't recognise it at first) a door was opened and to her immense surprise she recognised Mbogo.

"Hop in," he said with a laugh.

Startled, Mumbi hesitated.

"Come on, girlie," said Susan. Mumbi looked at her.

She was smiling in the moonlight. They drove away.

Since she had moved in it was her second night in the flat and she was again struck by its warmth and homely atmosphere. It was poorly furnished but much easier to keep tidy than the home she had left.

She went and sat on the bed. "It's so wonderful being here," she said, "It's a home."

Susan laughed, "Maybe you'll soon be tired of it."

"No!" said Mumbi, "Are you?"

"Well, one couldn't live here all one's life," Susan said, sitting next to her. "It's only low middle-class. Both our homes, let's face it, were low class. We have moved a step but it isn't enough. We must climb higher, somehow."

This is good enough for me, Mumbi thought. I could live here all my life.

"Where does Mbogo live?" she asked, remembering the man.

"I don't know," Susan admitted. "Probably Lumumba," she sighed. "Now he will move. An African location isn't the place for a man of his position. He'll have move to west or Parklands where the Asians live. And then to —"

"He isn't boss yet," Mumbi interrupted. "You don't even know he will be."

Susan smiled.

"We shall see," she said.

But Mumbi's doubts, even though they sprang from her prejudice, proved right. The next boss in the sales office turned out to be a young man they knew only slightly from another department. Both girls breathed with relief. Life under Mbogo would have been a difficult proposition. But Paul Chembwa was a nice idiot.

"I wonder how Mbogo feels." Mumbi remarked. "He had his covetous eye on the job."

"To be honest I am sorry for him," Susan said. "He works so hard. He was really the best man for the job. He is one of the unlucky ones like me. How long are we going to toil?"

"Don't worry," Mumbi said sympathetically. "Lots of changes are taking place around here. Maybe some luck will come your way."

Susan looked at her with large sombre eyes

"If I were to do this dreary work all my life, if I were to stick at grade five all my life — I guess I'd just die inside," she said.

But if ever the process commenced inside her there was no indication of it in the months that followed. In that period there was the sensational promotion of Mbogo to a peak post in the City offices. It hit the newspaper headlines. But to the two girls it wasn't such a shock.

"Good riddance," they agreed with satisfaction. And that seemed to be the general feeling in the sales office.

But if the girls thought they had seen the last of Mbogo they were mistaken. His job called for occasional visits to the industrial area branch. During these they could witness, not without envy, his speedy establishment into the more affluent strata of society. Once when he had come on one of these vsits he had driven them home, and later they had to admit to themselves that it was a treat.

Life was not exactly as Mumbi had hoped it would be. Only very occasionally did the gorgeous picture of city life as painted for her by Susan shine in real life. Nights could be dreary, especially later on when Susan was away for most of them. Here, right in the middle of the crowd she could be lonely — so lonely. She had a feeling of being closed in and often yearned for the freedom and the fresh air of the coutryside. Soon she had only one consolation — she was learning about life and to stand on her own. It would not have been so bad if Susan didn't leave her all alone in the flat when she went for dates. Sometimes when she came back her eyes were red and she smelt of liquor. Once Mumbi remarked on it and asked her not to drink so much. Susan stared at her stupidly and denied heatedly that she was drunk.

"But Susan," Mumbi said in a shocked voice, "anybody can smell it!"

"Smell what?"

"Beer, you have taken beer!"

Susan threw back her head and laughed.

"Don't be stupid," she said. "Why didn't you say that? Taken beer, yes. Positive. But drunk, not me. I'm not drunk."

"Where have you been?"

Susan laughed again and Mumbi was struck by the stupidity of her own question. What right had she to interfere? Perhaps she was too naive and inexperienced. Susan was so grown up and confident of herself. Maybe she knew what she was doing.

"Please don't think ill of me, Susan," she said, "It's only that I'm so lonely when you are gone and I become a little angry. I'm sorry."

Susan's face clouded. "I could ask you to come," she said in a gentle voice, "but I always feel you might not fit in."

Mumbi looked down. She swallowed a lump in her throat. "I understand," she said.

Susan took her hand, "Maybe you think I've been thoughtless," she said. "I know you do. But there have been reasons why I have left you out..."

Mumbi disengaged her hand. Bitterness flamed in her mind. She couldn't trust herself to speak. And what was there for her to say?

But that same night all the bitterness ebbed out of her, giving way to pity. In the night she was awakened by whispers from Susan beside her. In the darkness she silently listened.

"Nasty, nasty beast..." Susan gasped between sobs, "Nasty beast!" She tossed and turned in the bed in an agony of mind.

Mumbi lay awake, bewildered and cold.

Two days later Susan introduced her to Chege and Ken. The boys had been casual friends of Susan but as soon as Mumbi entered the picture the four paired off and the friendship warmed up fast. For Mumbi a new epoch seemed to have opened.

In the boys' car — an old black model they jointly owned — they went around town visiting night spots. For the first time she entered all the places she had heard Susan mentioning. On those occasions she felt a warm feeling of exhilaration and expectancy in her breast. She was on the threshold of life, exploring all its nooks and crannies. She was glad to have such wonderful friends to help her along. Chege and Ken were nice and polite and equally thirsty for fun and excitement. She was delighted to discover they had only left school a year before and were really just gaining experience like herself. Sometimes they disappeared for a few weeks and the girls knew that their money had run out. Always they came back.

When they were not around misery flooded in. Susan went out to meet other friends Mumbi never met. Mumbi would not fit in, she always said. Once she disappeared a whole long weekend.

She returned late on Sunday evening. She came in silently and at once Mumbi felt that something was wrong.

"I'd given you up." Mumbi said, "Where have you been? Home?"

Susan made a poor attempt at a smile, "Home? No."

"Is anything wrong?"

"No — nothing is wrong." Then she turned and smiled. "I think I'll — I'll be lucky at last," she said.

"What do you mean?"

"I'll be a secretary..."

"Really! Oh Susan..." Mumbi impulsively went to embrace her but something checked her. "I'm happy for you," she said.

Why was there that awkward feeling between them? What was wrong? Something was.

"I was making some coffee. Would you like some?" Mumbi ventured.

"Yes. Black please," Susan replied wearily. She sank on the bed and lay looking at the ceiling. Mumbi looked at her and understood. For some reason she was not shocked. She just wondered. It couldn't be Ken.

"Black?" she said. "Funny."

Susan made no reply. She seemed too tired to talk. Mumbi went into the kitchen and added more water in the pot. She came back.

"How did you hear the good news? You must have made an awful secret of it." She reflected a little bitterly that Susan had kept so many other secrets from her. "When were you interviewed?"

"There was no interview," Susan said in a flat, dry voice.

"Really! Well, who told you?"

There was a pause. "Mbogo." Susan said weakly.

Mumbi stiffened. "Mbogo! But he...!"

Susan turned and stared emptily at her.

"He is a nasty, n-a-s-t-y beast ..." she said her voice trembling.

Mumbi walked to the bed and sat on the edge of it. She took Susan's hand and pressed it. Their eyes held for a moment and then Susan broke into tears.

There really was no need for Susan to talk — to confess. But Mumbi let her sob it out. She listened and squeezed her hand.

fifteen

the hill

It is not a significant hill. In fact if the land below did not lie so flat, this projection of nine acres or so would go unnoticed. But it is as if God had designed that it should stand out naked, and with it Old Kibonde who owns these acres of virtual nothingness, a grass thatched hut up near the top, and a few sheep and cattle which ought to have died off owing to starvation but haven't. From a distance the hut is to be seen dotted, pinned, confined permanently to this hill as people travel along the road leading to the market. The road is some distance from the foot of the hill, cutting a straight but dusty way to the west, as if in a perpetual hurry to cut the shortest distance between two points (the village and the market) or, perhaps, to give Old Kibonde's hill a wide berth, a cold shoulder.

Old Kibonde feels secluded but conspicuous.

To the east there is the steep river where the ghost of his son lies. The river brushes its fertile bank along the dry foot of the hill and its age-old deposits of fertile soil groom tall Kikuyu grass perpetually green as if to mock Old Kibonde's scorched hill. Over the years — no one around can tell when — some of the water has curved its insidious arm around the entire hill, surrounding it, so that Old Kibonde can jolly well consider his possession of nine acres an island if he likes.

No one else cares, and he feels the encircling water with the forceful reality of a large knot around the neck.

True to the geography of the area, the wind almost always blows from east to west. It seems to have declared war now and has combed dry the eastern slopes of the hill, quite often hurling angry dust across to the other side, on to the hut — if not occasionally playing darts with his ageing eyes.

But if all this casts a shadow upon the twilight days of the old man, he does nonetheless present a cheerful face in resignation.

Although they say he's gone funny in the head, that's only hearsay and you should not believe it. For one punged with certain inarticulate questions tickling at his mind like the surface, yet intimate, scratch of pins it is conceivable that he might occasionally behave slightly quietly. But to the visitor who drops in, or up, to pay regards, the tourist who dons hat and binoculars to see the land below, the surveyor who mounts fields glasses at the top for vantage, or the occasional picnic party, the old man leaves an impression of genuine and sane hospitality; or seems at least to suffer the intrusion with cheerful indifference.

But the shadow is there. In the evening the setting sun impresses a beautiful if apprehensive warmth on the western part of the hill as the old man sits on a stool outside his hut dipping his finger into a snuff box. He presses the snuff into his nostril and breathes it in. Then, as has been his habit lately, he rubs his two hands together as if caressing the sunset, knowing very well it is slowly, inevitably, withdrawing beyond the horizon. The eastern slopes behind his back gather shadow rapidly towards a chilling night, like a distant and blotted past, better forgotten.

As he sits there outside the hut seemingly thinking nothing in particular, his mind wanders into a wilderness and finally settles on a particular thought with a jerk. The old man accordingly digs his buttocks into the bowl of the stool, uncomfortably. The ghost of the past has once again caught up with him and his mind after wandering evasively has once again settled, imprisoned upon a centre, a thought, the indelible scratch which has been his conscience these past ten years.

It is always like that. Whenever he is alone he deliberately tries to face the reality that his past is virtually unknown to the society around him — beyond the fact that years ago he deserted his wife and son — and he must forget.

After all he is not the first man who has fled matrimony.

But his thoughts are like scattered kites wandering round and round in the air, only to settle down eventually at the mercy of the little boy's imprisoning hand where they started.

* * *

He had married a long time before as a young man. Although the missionaries had arrived with new techniques and the local pastor insisted on less violent means, Kibonde had considered the old approach more exciting and his girlfriend was dragged home by his friends. But as soon as his father settled the dowry, Kibonde ran away. He had heard that some of his friends were making a fortune in town. Those were the days when the white man had introduced the rupee and the sound of coins singing in young men's pockets became something to shout about.

Something in him warned that he might not return. But Kibonde was Kibonde and not just any other scoundrel, he argued to himself. So, in the manner of any young man going away, he promised Njeri and their young son that he would come back soon and left, cleanly.

He had always approached most things in life, women and marriage not excepted, in a kind of high spirited fashion. He soon found the city conducive to this. Any promises he might have made to Njeri began to take on a distant ring.

His first job was at a hotel nick-named the 'Smiths Aboad' where the manager kicked him for a fortnight. He was soon made to understand that Nairobi may have been a bush town in a wild jungle but dinner jackets and bowties were to be insisted upon before any customer dined there.

But the clients kicked their way in too.

He picked up his swahili fast (ndiyo, bwana). Then a few months later, his opportunity to become a house servant where he would at least be kicked by only one man instead of several, waddled in one morning in the shape of a stocky European whom he had seen several times at the 'Smiths Aboad'.

Boy! said Big Man, Mr. Jones, sitting legs askew, tummy sticking out.

Bwana!

Lete kahawa

Ndiyo, Bwana

Kibonde brought the coffee, after which Big Man Mr. Jones grabbed him confidentially by the neck. He brought Kibonde's ear level to his mouth. Kibonde's forehead rested upon the table, bottom sticking out as if requesting the cane.

Listen.

Ndiyo, bwana!

How would you like to work for Big Man?

Which man, bwana?

Me, *pumbavu*. I'll increase your salary by twenty cents.

But Kifagio will not let me.

Kifagio?

My manager.

No, I know he would only kick you. Not that I won't. I'll pay you this month's salary. Are you married?

Mm — No!

Fine, fine now! (slapping him across the bottoms). Pack up. One more thing —

Bwa—

Any nicknames for me or memsahib and —...

They were not bad people, the Jones. Apart from the fact that the equally big memsahib had a bad temper in the morning and inspected the house suspiciously always finding out what he was up to with the butter, Kibonde could boast more peace of mind than most houseboys. It is true that it took him time to get used to washing other people's underwear and he occasionally made a mess of the breakfast egg which he was quite often dying to eat. It is also true that Jones lived up to his promise and kicked him whenever he felt like stretching his legs for exercise. But weighed against screams that issued from other houses in the neighbourhood, life with the Jones' was good.

Besides, the Jones, who were childless but made up for the fact by keeping a dog (George) and a cat (Pati), seemed in need of a fifth party in the evening who would at least stand there on two legs and listen and say 'yes', and not ask any questions. Sometimes they would ask him about himself in between yawns. But they would hardly be bothered with his past. Nevertheless he could not restrain the feeling that their asking him about himself was in itself a great honour.

He felt uneasy about deserting his wife. Once or twice an old friend passing by would tickle his conscience by mentioning Njeri and their little boy Mbara, and Kibonde would give him some money to take 'back home'. But he could never be sure that these old friends were not hungry loafers who never went home anyway. As a matter of fact Njeri soon became very remote in his memories. As a town man he gradually came to consider himself rather advanced for her and would rather make love to the nannies in the neighbourhood who at least wore rubber shoes. Her beads and Kikuyu ornaments may have been suitable for the up country bum. But they would not become the wife of a gentleman who wore starched khaki and who had now acclimatised his feet to the smooth concrete of the Jones' floor.

Njeri would never, he knew, change her traditional ways.

Bwana na memsahib sometimes went away and only the dog barked at him and ruled the house by wagging its tail. On such occasions, as soon as the pets were fully fed he would take advantage of the breathing space to sneak off to some friend. None of them would believe him when he said he had actually *sat* in the living room the previous night with Bwana and Memsahib.

No wonder he speaks English so well!

No wonder he knows so much about England!

Naturally, it would not have been like Kibonde not to exaggerate a little. But his state was nevertheless enough cause for envy by other house servants. Their only consolation was that they at least had not betrayed their wives.

They would gather together as he strolled away majestically and paint the picture worse than the reports had shown it.

But if Kibonde was happier than most servants, his fortunes were drastically reversed when one afternoon he threw memsahib's cat into the bath. At least that was Mrs. Jones version of the 'Wet Cat Story'. It was of course the only version that mattered and it went round the neighbourhood for a week.

It need hardly be said that Kibonde found himself thrown out of the house that evening after several years' service — screamed at by Mrs. Jones, kicked by Jones and chased well beyond the gate by George.

2

Through the twigs and leaves of the bamboo and blue gum trees stole the fresh moonlight, caressing Njeri's hair and the beads of wood and copper around her neck and waist. She sat still save for the occasional lift of a hand to brush off a tear drop, brooding as she stared pensively into the river. She was about twenty eight and looked every bit a married mother of two, which she wasn't but had always wanted to be. From arm's length she coolly regarded the water which flowed silently except for slight splashing sounds as it whirled softly round to curve shallow ripples.

Now and then the bubbling resentment within her would burst, and then she plunged pebbles into the river with the unconscious desire to break the silvery reflection. Break and if possible annihilate the moon itself; for it seemingly mocked her as it stole sparkling reflections everywhere: on her oily ornamented legs, on the bangles around her hands and ankles, and on the tear drops silently but steadily welling down her cheeks which, when otherwise provoked into a smile, formed beautiful dimples.

It made her feel she was in her teens and in love, the first of which she wasn't and the best we can say of the second is that she had been in love once with a coward or cheat who had dragged her into marriage and then ran off. True, Kibonde had promised to return. But that was a long time ago and he had forsaken her, no doubt for a modern girl with lipstick.

"Within a short time," he had said gaily, "I'll be back for you. Just let me settle down." But her youth was swiftly drifting away. He might have dragged her to his hut eight years ago but if he thought he could drag her to the city in search of him, then she wasn't Ngumi's daughter.

It was when she had sat there by the river for two hours that she resolved to ignore her father's warning. She would go it alone and see the medicine man. She had gone back to her father, who now claimed that the dowry was far from being paid by Kibonde's family. In short, he had little faith in the ability of "that clan" to keep a wife.

* * *

He was famous and popularly nicknamed Mwara. For he was clever, if also cunning, and there wasn't a herb in the medicine world that he could not lecture to you on from daybreak to mid-day if you had the patience. He knew your ills as soon as you stepped into his hut and hardly had you sat down than he shot a few spots of the correct *muthaiga* down your throat. Then, rubbing his canny hands together, he shot you one threatening look from behind long eyelashes as a silent warning that the only thing that now remained was a small goat for the witchdoctor's pains. No one dared forget.

Old men saw him about their ailing sight. Superstitious characters consulted him on how best to avoid *thahu* and the misfortunes in store for them as a result of tempting the wheels of fortune by such unforgiveable acts as passing under the long stick supporting the banana plant. Mothers took their toddlers along for prescriptions or blessings and all paid heed to his word. And when the day for religious rite under the revered fig tree came, they all saw in his ageing, hard, almost cruel eyes moral inspiration for the eternal war which everyone waged against the evil spirits, to hell with the local pastor's warning.

It was of course in matters of love that his esteem stood at an unmatched peak. And this was not the first time Mwara was going to deal with the sobs of a self-pitying, despairing girl whose husband had run off.

"So you've come at last?" Mwara asked, very white-haired and diminutive, almost unworldly. "Your father is of course a domineering, sceptical and stingy old jigger in whose company I've enjoyed nothing but spite, but I, I never bear a grudge... no, not old Mwara."

"Father did not know about this," Njeri said.

"In and out they still come to Mwara's hut despite your father's scandalising tongue. In and out, in and out .... even you now."

"I said father did not know I was coming here." Njeri clenched her hands together, a little angry, a little ashamed.

"He didn't? Oh, well, never mind. To business at hand. To business... a matter I knew would come up... just a matter of time!" Mwara was half singing it now and it gave Njeri a queer feeling inside. It was as if she was offering herself for sacrifice. She had heard the tune before. The goat killer always sang it during sacrifice.

Mwara went into the hut. She silently followed. She could see nothing at first. It was all dark, so coldly strange.

"Sick man's stool!" Mwara shouted from an inner chamber, unconcerned. She looked round and at last found it. There was utter silence as between sworn enemies, none of whom wanted to start a quarrel.

"So you want another husband? Are you sure Kibonde is never coming back ... but you must be. That kind never returns. Not that I didn't warn you when your father turned us down. Said my first son wasn't good enough... phew!"

Then from the inner room there came a sudden clatter of metals, then a sound as of two knives grinding in cruel roughness against each other. Njeri all but fled outside. After a still longer and even colder silence, Mwara emerged with a small round goat-skin bag, the size of the thumb, to which was attached a leather string.

He was smiling .... so warmly in fact that after a few undecided moments she was soon smiling back.

"Take this good-luck charm and wear it round your waist. When you see the man you want, quickly take it off and hang it around your neck. You will find he will come sweeping you into his arms faster than a whirlpool. And this time," he added, "he won't slip through like a liar."

Mwara rubbed his small hands.

Farther down the path leading away from the dilapidated hut which overlooked the hill, Njeri stopped to admire her lightly-packed talisman. It had a bitter-sweet, pungent smell and was rather heavy for its size. It seemed all so potent and powerful, ready to fill the air with its odour. Njeri looked at it seriously.

"This either does it," she said, "or nothing will."

Indeed it worked. Exactly six days later she brought

Mwangi to her father's house to introduce him to the family. Here was a man who would never run off. The sun was already burying its hard gold of twilight over the hill to make way for a big lover's moon sailing a silvery way softly in the east. She left her lover with her father while she strolled away in optimistic restlessness. She was sure he would make a good impression. He was strong and intelligent and had promised to treat her son Mbara like his own. Surely that was her father's idea of a man?

Then it happened. Inside her father's hut there came sounds of heavy pounding and thundering, stools clashing and pots smashing. Somebody was being knocked against the wall repeatedly, and large lumps of the earthern wall were disintegrating on the outside.

Njeri rushed towards the hut in time to behold her suitor ejected through the small door. She raised cries of protest as Mbara clutched at her with a stolen yam in one hand. Then she saw Mwara's small body shoot out as well. Her father followed, carrying a large stick, breathing hard.

"Don't kill us," pleaded Mwara. "Don't kill my son!"

"Get going, you double-crossing little owl," Njeri's father shouted. "You bring that second son of yours to court my daughter for my wealth again and I'll flay you nailed to your fig-tree."

Njeri dug her hand under the soft cloth around her waist. She found the talisman, its smell still powerful and pungent, yet so impotent.

Then, furiously, she sent it flying away.

3

Whether Kibonde had in fact thrown the cat into the steaming bath and nearly maimed the dog; whether he had always talked political holocaust to the other servants as Mrs. Jones was now saying by the end of the second week to pep up the bored neighbourhood — is not important. It does not matter either that the Society for the Prevention of Cruelty to Animals had also been notified. But Kibonde's attitude changed bitterly. As he kept looking for work elsewhere, he could not help feeling that this was a stáb in the back. He had not only tolerated the Jones' platitudes and obsession with animals but he had been more faithful to their pets than to his wife. He had dutifully cleared the cat's and dog's dirt without grumbling, though any true Kikuyu would have thrashed hell out of the animals each time they messed the backyard. And, for thanks, even the dog had bitten him in the backside.

One of these days he was going to kill somebody.

But he eventually found a job as a house servant to a batchelor. Mr. Martin wasn't too fastidious about domestics and rarely cared in what state his breakfast egg emerged from the kitchen. And he had no pets. In fact he treated Kibonde with more humanity than was safe. For Kibonde felt that such freedom as he was given by Bwana Martin could only lead to disaster. He might over-step it at a point difficult to tell and then he would be kicked out or worse. A white man was a white man and you could take too much liberty in those days. In fact for a while it was worse than a house with pets. But he was soon reassured. He thanked God there was no woman in the house, and although Christianity and himself had parted company as soon as they had made acquaintance, what his village preacher once called Adam's wife in a moment of passion was the only thing Kibonde could now take seriously. He now applied this to Njeri for self-excuse and blamed all his previous troubles on Mrs. Jones.

It was therefore with a mixture of shock, surprise and I-just-don't-know-what-to-think that he heard this from Mr. Martin one evening:

Kibonde!

Bwana —

Soon there will be three of us.

Bwana?

You, me and a memsahib.

Bw — bwana!

To Kibonde, Mr. Martin was not the marrying kind — any more than he himself was. Well, there was a point of identification! Mr. Martin did of course bring a girl to the house occasionally and Kibonde would make the bedroom tidy. But by and large bwana sat at home in the evenings, reading or teaching Kibonde some English, something other servants never believed.

But now, Kibonde thought almost bitterly, there was the prospect of another Mrs. Jones.

4

Mbara, the son of Njeri, grew into a strong believer in the might of the law. Whether it was women's jewels or his neighbour's shirt, the odds were that the law had the last and louder laugh. Perhaps this was his big advantage over amateur actors in the trade ever since he ran away from home. Where men of lesser judgement trespassed the law on impulse, he himself calculated. He would not lose sight of the fact that men like him trod the long carpet of the law which the police seemed to pull unexpectedly from under their feet.

He never grabbed things over the counter or played you a nasty trick, until he had looked up and down the street to make sure that there was no policeman at hand, or a special branch man in sheep's clothing.

This does not mean that Mbara, who like his father Kibonde came to forget home, never had his rainy day. True enough his judgement was bound to falter. On a few occasions in those unpredictable fifties the Bench was confronted with the case of Regina versus Mbara. But our defendant viewed this in the pragmatic light of good experience.

"After all," he would confide to his colleague acquaintances — for real friends he never made — "it can't all be clear waters. There will be spells of unpredictable storms. Besides, we must be acquainted with the calibre of the men on the other side."

His colleagues were spivs who had been thrown to it by circumstances. One of his more intimate ones was Mungai whose mother had died when he was less than a year old. His father had been lured by the white man into the Second World War. He joined the King's African Rifles and went to Burma. The last anybody ever heard was that he died — for the Empire and Crown — a brave man. But by and large for Mbara, business was going 'straight'.

Having started 'humbly' back home in the reserves, in so far as the word can be cautiously extended to his profession, he became one of the shrewd few who had done well in the thriving, if hazardous, preoccupation of robbing the rich. At a time when many children of his age worked themselves to bits over big chunks of vernacular: Adam and Eve, Jonah and the Whale; at a time when the illusions and delusions of his friend Chege and others as policemen or even clergymen were the rule: Mbara was being practical. Buttons were missing off his classmate's pants and pins from girl's hair. Then as Mbara realised his ambition further, the headmaster came in one morning to report that someone (not putting it beyond the capability of some in the class) had polefished his trousers.

Those were the days when Mbara foresaw himself as a future mastermind of the big rackets. But he had hardly laid the foundation. On at least one occasion his pace of progress suffered a setback when the teacher, who had been turned down by Njeri twice since Kibonde disappeared, awarded him splashes of the cane, ordering him to run round the field each morning for two weeks. (Which was in a way good training because later on Mbara did run frequently from the laws of His Majesty's Government.)

Needless to say he never got far with school and all the irrelevant handicap of its curriculum, although being a calculating man he would have done well at arithmetic. What he termed the "impediment of rural vulgarity" stood between him and his intended career. Like his father Kibonde, whom he could never remember and whom he would have strangled on sight, he had to move to the City to tap new ground. He knew that everyone — perhaps with the exception of his long-suffering classmates — would object to such plans. He should, therefore, steal away without letting even his mother know.

In a way, he felt his only friend Chege did not deserve this, for they both liked each other very much. However, Mbara simply let himself into his grandfather's house through the window, collected the bag of money from under the pillow, and set out secretly along the road to the city.

5

Kibonde was still quite happy despite Mr. Martin's marriage. Mrs. Martin was barely old enough, if you asked Kibonde's opinion, and he would not have put it beyond

Mr. Martin to have dragged her home against her mother's will. The disparity in age was considerable. Mr. Martin soon began buying more and more books, read the *Illustrated London News* regularly, and kept his eye on the Honours List at Buckingham Palace. Mrs. Martin became more frustrated, not being the intellectual type, and bought herself a cat which she fondled. Kibonde became worried. Perhaps she wanted children. In fact, Kibonde, who over the years had now picked up sufficient English to be able to come to sensible conclusions between the pauses in the Englishman's bedroom conversation, sensed a quarrel one evening when washing dishes, and putting his ear to the keyhole, made out words to that effect.

It was then that he tossed in bed all night and wondered about memsahib's behaviour lately. Once or twice when bwana was off to work, she had told him to fix a pin here or there on her hair and dress, to rub her back a little or to straighten the seams of her stockings, what did it mean? He shuddered to think what the white man's government would do to him if he were to be found 'molesting' a white woman. But he had heard that some servants —.

Kibonde tightened in horror, kicked at the blankets, and told himself not to be silly. Here he was, a man who had deserted his own wife, thinking unforgivable thoughts. Was it not enough that he had whispered bold sacrilege into the ears of the ayahs around? No sooner would he hear of a new nanny fresh from the village than he would seek acquaintance. At first, of course, he would take the news apprehensively and ask what she looked like. Then his face melted into a smile as he concluded that it couldn't be Njeri. ('This one is too black. We'll have to use some of memsahib's powder.')

But it was not true. Mrs. Martin did not become more suggestive. And although he had dreaded it and spent sleepless nights, now that she did not encourage him he felt snubbed and disappointed. Would it not have been a kind of revenge on Mrs. Jones, after all?

Bwana and memsahib moved to a new house with a swimming pool. The waters sent a chill through Kibonde. It was as if some of his past was burried in the dark depths, and every time he looked at it his head went round and round. A major quarrel broke out in the house. It couldn't have been about the cat although Kibonde had begun packing just in case. Soon afterwards Mr. Martin took to drinking, the books gathered dust and a divorce followed. Mrs. Martin took the cat. For a year Kibonde lived a life of fear and packed up once or twice when bwana came in with a bunch of letters. Mrs. Martin might send a conciliatory letter saying her only condition was not to keep a servant who had seen her go.

But things became better, if anything, although Mr. Martin drank more. Then the middle-aged bwana began frequenting night clubs. He quarrelled in the morning with each call girl he brought the previous night from Gino's. Some were black, some the colour of milk chocolate. Kibonde was a little envious and lusted for the milk chocolate ones whom he thought more civilised as they sat in the soft light of the living room with Mr. Martin's arm around them. Mr. Martin, sensing this, laughed at him. But just in case Kibonde spread the news to the neighbours, Mr. Martin raised his trusted servant's salary four times in the following months, so that things took a turn for the worse.

6

Whenever the woman stopped, the child stopped too. And, for a time at least, the trail of brown dust which their feet excited would come to an end. The two would sit down to rest at the road side, the woman staring blankly into the distant waste of horizon ahead. Even when resting, they could get no shade. The child would hold on to his mother's dress with an expression which betrayed confusion, wonder and hunger. Occasionally he would call, "mother . . . mother."

He would get no answer, and though she knew what he wanted, he would get no food.

Then, after a while, they would resume their tired journey. He would fall in behind, marking double steps to keep up with her and holding fast on to the hem of her bleached dress as if afraid she might slip away even in such broad daylight. While the tail of his oversize khaki shirt thinly brushed the soft surface of the road, the thumb of his free hand would be in his mouth. He sucked and sucked, until it was clean of dust and dirt. Then he would transfer the hem into this hand to suck the other thumb clean. This way he occupied himself, staring the while somewhere between the ground and the hem in his hand. Now and then he heard his mother begin talking to herself, unintelligibly. And, apprehensively he would ask, "Mother . . . . mother . . . . what is the matter?"

He never got any answer. He might as well have asked for a cake.

The sun had crept on across the sky and now it was overhead. And like this sun which had risen so rapidly but now marked slowed, deliberate steps as mid-day came in, their movement too had become laborious. To the occasional stranger on the hot road, the two looked a haggard sight. As the heat beat down upon them too benevolently, salty sweat dripped down their bodies. The woman's dress accordingly clung at the moist back and underarms, and the boy's large, loose shirt stuck uncomfortably, flapping. He wore no shorts.

Beyond the visible mile of the unending road ahead, a mirage which they could not hope to reach rippled and shimmered with mocking, tantalising moistness.

The fatherless child could not have been more than five years old. At any rate, the world bewildered him. The wide, dusty road which climbed up to the horizon over the hills only to roll down again promised no end. And his mother would say nothing to him beyond admonishing him for sucking his thumb at his age.

She on the other hand could not be less than thirty years old. It was now more than twelve years since Kibonde had deserted her. Although she had decided to stay in the reserves, she had now considerably changed her attitude towards 'the new ways'. After all, the missionaries had done their duty throughout the country as only true servants of God could. Mwara, the witchdoctor, for instance, had been locked up years ago and his hut burnt down as an example.

As the child trotted behind her now after so many years, she could not tell whether she was in fact on the right road. But all roads led to the City and it was only a blind man who could miss it. Worse still, she did not know what she would do once she got there. But one thing she did know was that she would not look for Kibonde. The child trotting behind her was her second and, to say the least, a cause of more misery than she had even had. She had not married again. Mbara, her first son, had run off to the City in his father's lamentable style and the latest she had heard was that he was in constant conflict with the law, and was 'changing jails like shirts'.

Now she herself seemed to have no alternative. She had become the laughing stock at home for even her youngest sister had comfortably settled down with a man. She could not bear it. She was still beautiful, that much she could tell. Well, they said that was enough for Nairobi. If she couldn't get a job decent enough for a woman who couldn't write her own name, then there was *that* to turn to. . . . .

"Mother . . . . mother . . . ."

"Shut up!"

7

How he survived his first six years in the City surprised Mbara, on reflection, as much as everyone else including the police. But somehow or other, he wedged his way up amidst the tribulations of the law's baton and the hostility of Holier-than-thou citizens. In seven years he waded his way through from part-time shoe-shine boy, pick-pocket and pedlar to professional robber with his alias once in the black books at the police headquarters. He never heard of his father, any more than he cared to.

It was not all easy hitch-hiking. Many a man who worked with him and landed their failure in jail, won his antagonism when they said he had it easy to the top.

"The only job where you bang in from the top, you fools, is digging a hole," he would say.

Even then you dug, laboured to get somewhere, to sink all the way into the underworld. In any case, he saw his profession as the bottom of a hole. He often said that in his job you started off with a character, a conscience, then you dug your hole down, moulding and hardening your character, and burying your conscience deeper and deeper. When you got *there* you were bereft of all sentiment. But it was evident that Mbara himself had not got there yet, though he made out he had. Although he never killed, owing to a trace of conscience, he felt he might be forced to it soon. Every time he considered the possibility, however, the feeling came to him that it might mean his end. As for robbery, he could rob anyone except the church, firstly because churches reminded him of his formidable village priest in which case he convinced himself that churches had no money anyway; but chiefly because he superstitiously believed there was a limit, providence's red line, and an act of trespass would get him kicked off the cliff's edge.

Mbara spent a further prosperous two years treating his criminal palate to the taste of motor car tyres, other people's bank accounts and office typewriters. He had already begun warming his hand to wholesale, indiscriminate blackmail when the ring of the might of law came clamouring in his ears.

It was one evening when a sudden storm fell and swept in floods one foot high. Mbara was waiting along with other people for it to clear when he caught sight of a policeman. The latter had been moving up and down the street but now he stood looking at Mbara rather suspiciously.

There was something about the youthful policeman which made Mbara uneasy. It was as if the policeman's carriage, something in his arrogant gait and build, carried connotations of rude familiarity. Had they met before?

"Excuse me," he said moving over to Mbara.

But Mbara was not going to wait. He had met, during his career, policemen who approached him in the same friendly fashion and ended up asking him hostile questions about taxes.

"Please wait," the policeman said again.

Somehow the attention of the bystanders was attracted. To good society only waiting to go home in peace, Mbara could well be one of those who would take advantage of the storm to pick someone's pocket. But what mattered to this good society right then was that the law had extended its hand towards him.

Soon there was havoc, everyone was running after him. The policeman shouted to them to stop. But they did not.

Still running, Mbara drew out his knife. He hit out wildly. He missed. He hit out again. Then, as everyone stopped for the split moment of disbelief following the reality of the climax, Mbara made away and got lost in the rain.

That night, he found it hard to sleep. The conscience he thought he had lost as one who lived only for himself organising big rackets, nagged at him. He cursed himself for it. Was it not to be expected that in combat with the law, men would die on both sides?

But that thought was no comfort. The face of that particular policeman worried him. He would clear out of the City, travelling as ordinarily as possible. When the wave of mass hunts by the police ended, he would return.

He stepped out of the bus and stood hesitantly by the road. Even after so many years, he could not fail to recognise his grandfather's house. Dilapidated it was; but its aura of take-it-or-leave-it pride had survived the physical weight of years. Its new corrugated iron roof looking grotesque on old walls, proclaimed loud rays of the evening sun which a rain cloud was trying to threaten beyond the hill.

It was as if nothing could touch it. All told Mbara clearly that his absence had not made any difference any more than the scandalous behaviour of his father had. He wondered what his mother was now really like. Why he did not know. But it did seem strange that as the bus rattled into the country-side, he should have felt any attachment to his childhood.

Perhaps it was the serenity of the deep air, unlike the urban shallow stuff, which felt nostalgic. The only son of his mother — as far as he knew — he had not seen her since he robbed her father.

He thought of the colleagues whom he alienated rather than befriended. When in trouble, he had been able to fall back on no one although he did fall back on the police quite often when he made a false move. They seemed to be the only ones glad to have him, if only on their own terms.

Would anyone respond to his arrival favourably? Many a time he had felt that he ought to come home, make his mother believe that he had been doing respectably well; he would marry and not desert like his father, he promised. Still, was it too late?

All of a sudden as he stood there in a white suit, Mbara felt that his return was reminiscent of a Sunday School lesson long ago. Why the chapter of the prodigal son should have flown into his mind, Mbara could not tell. For to him, that lesson had only held a personal triumph.

Slowly, he now picked his way down the path which threaded through his grandfather's large farm. His feet raised storms of dust one foot high, powdering its dry-brown on his white trousers and shoes. Mbara remembered the flood and shuddered.

As he came nearer and crossed the river, he discovered many more people than he expected on such a day. Was it a feast? But a feast of what nature? Then as he approached still nearer, anxiety swept over him and he hurried. There was nothing exuberant in this, nothing happy about the gathering. It could mean only one thing. Someone was dead.

Soon he joined the crowd. He won the attention of the priest conducting the funeral ceremony, the priest lost his audience, and all eyes turned on the white suit. No one seemed to recognise the newcomer. Mbara felt his heart race. Was it his mother?

"You viper!" the priest shouted. He was dressed in black save for his collar which clung round his neck in white impeccability. Standing on top of a high table for strategy, he comfortably looked down at his audience, and they quite uncomfortably looked up at him. As if to admit his perennal heavenly magic over his sinning earthly audiences, the crowd agitated. As usual, however collectively, they could only stir a mute defence. Mbara recognised the metallic Sunday School severity of the voice.

"Repent now! So that when this body ... this greed ... this earthen flesh ... this dirt ... buries in its own! Your soul! Will find a seat! In the Kingdom of the Maker!"

Mbara went weak at the knee. He tried to control himself. He touched the old woman who stood in front of him. She turned. Before he could speak, she clutched at him.

"Oh, sir, he was such a nice young man. Now he is gone." He recognised her as Chege's mother, his childhood playmate.

"I always warned him not to be a policeman. Not in that cruel City."

Again, Mbara remembered the flood. He saw for a moment Chege's blood spout and splash into the current.

"You viper!"

He could wait no more. Slowly, he dragged himself amidst the solemn faces. Then he picked the path down towards the river at the foot of the hill.

In nostalgia, he stopped to look up at the sinking sun. As a child, he and Chege had loved to watch it sink over the hill. Now the sun was reluctantly yielding its twilight beyond the hill to the painful thunder of a storm cloud. Soon the cloud would spread. Then it would lower and shower its dark, wet wing on the silent roofs of a shocked village.

He would not suffer sunrise. Only he would wait for the storm and the flood.

8

The ring and chime of the Christmas bells at St. Mary's Cathedral carried through the calm, easy morning arrãyed with a bright sky, clearly and smoothly. It was a different day, pleasantly different. Surprisingly so, considering the clouds and the mist, the rain and the dampness of the past few days. Pedestrians and motorists whistled tunes which struck an undertone of optimism; hopeful that the blue sky here and there adorned with specks of milk-white, innocent clouds like Chirstmas icing, would mark up a pleasant day in their diaries.

Everyone, not to be outdone in the embrace of a morning fraught with brotherly greetings and radiant faces, joined in. The newspaper man in the booth sold, in between humming appropriate carols, more papers than any other day in the week. The Red Cross girl in a white blouse and cap and bearing a collection box, a coquetish smile and an expectant eye, cadged coins from the stingy Christians without any more effort than one coaxing look and "hallelujah, brother!" Twinkles of gold winked shyly from ladies' jewels in the sun as the soft breeze ruffled their skirts.

Kamau stopped by a Government Road music shop, scratched a bug out of his hair, and with the palm of the other hand beat at the flies which gave him no peace. He was barefooted and he wore a tattered shirt. His shorts had been tanned brown by dust, sweat and dirt. Two tears across the bottom put the final touch to the story. A look at his dark eyes revealed a shadow, almost haunted, and accentuated by rather long eyelashes. One read in that shadow uncertainty and apprehension for tomorrow, as if the world still bewildered him ever since his mother deserted him. He had then been about five years old. The only thing he could now remember was the way he had clung to her dress on that long road. When they reached the City, she bought him the biggest cake he had ever seen and that was the last he saw of her. The police had then tossed him into the hands of one charity home to another like a basket-ball and later this had alternated with turns at the reform schools.

He now stood, pensive, by the music store and scratched at his arm-pit, then at his hair again. Curly and very black, God had set it on his head with the meticulous hand of a sculptor who would rather discard the whole head than curve a hairline out of place. But now it had gone copper-brown. He scratched more furiously.

Lively music began playing from inside as if to taunt him, and two people laughed unproariously because life could be funny. A couple of children passed by toying with brightly coloured balloons. In fact life was fun. Across the street, bulbs and neon lights said Merry Christmas to him from a shop window. They advertised Uplands pork.

A chuckling, heavy drunken man with a beaded cap staggered towards him and said, "Want a merry Christmas fight lad?" and still chuckling, waddled away.

Kamau clenched his fist. He hated Christmas and he would like to strangle everybody, he said. His mother, that ruffian half brother Mbara whom he had heard of but never met, his father whoever that was and . . .

*13

By the stares directed at him, Kamau realised he was shouting. He also knew he must have smashed his fingers against the steel latch of the door for they were bleeding. What did it matter? There was pain enough in a starving belly, damn bleeding fingers.

He recollected himself and followed with his eyes a middle-aged woman who had stopped at the glass window. She had a large, full handbag. A painful moment gripped his mind and he hesitated. Then he noticed that the drunken man, no longer in chuckles, had come back and was gravely eyeing the handbag.

He might beat Kamau to it.

The two hours at the swimming pool had been crucial. It had not been Kamau's intention to come here but he did not know where he was going. He vaguely recalled running away. Even when out of reach, he had kept running as if in a day dream. At last he found himself at this pool which was well hidden except from the large house some yards away and which evidently belonged to the same owner.

He stared at the water, coolly, almost unafraid. Its soft rippling beckoned him with a calmness that was so irreconcilable to the distant atmosphere at the music store. The sun reflected in the water and reached out its shattered fingers to him to reassure and invite, menacingly.

Faintly, weakly, he tossed the handbag into the water. Then, submitting, he leapt in after it.

9

She stood there, waiting for him to say something, to talk to her. He wasn't a great talker, at least not where women were concerned. Most of the time he would just sit there in a quiet corner, drinking or sipping his beer, indifferent to everyone. Every now and then he would shout for more pilsner and the waiter would drift across mechanically like a live dummy. This was usually in the evenings after a dog's day at the office. In fact his had become a dog's life. He had now long forgotten that the Honours List existed at Buckingham Palace, or wherever it was. Even he could not see how a man who had let the side down so scandalously and who in the past few years had switched to several jobs could be recommended by the Governor. As a matter of fact, there had been talk lately of shipping him back home quietly as a poor example of an Englishman abroad. It was unacceptable for instance to those who frequented the "Smiths Aboad" that a friend who had once been tipped as possible Chief Secretary could now have sunk so low that his house servant was the virtue ruler of the house.

Of course Mr. Martin would have thrown Kibonde right out if he had chosen to. But the neighbours had to talk about something.

Mr. Martin sat there at the corner and asked himself what he would do if it were not for Kibonde. There was something about the 'house boy' that remained very loyal, if slightly cynical and self assured lately, which Mr. Martin could not risk with another servant. It would be like self exposure. There had been established between the two a certain kind of mutual dependence while at the same time the roles of master and servant were furtively upheld.

They were both about fifty now. Kibonde, who continued to make love to neighbouring nannies with a laxity that was hard to believe, was convinced that bwana would not marry again. The first lesson, now better forgotten, had been good enough. Everything about the house ran smoothly if not to convention, and the neighbours had been defied quite successfully over the years.

The man's morality had now scraped rock bottom, they said. Every established tart in town must have known his bed, and some violence in the morning if she was exorbitant. The neighbours were in fact very angry.

Now, as he sat in a corner at the Equator, Mr. Martin wondered what had really gone wrong. But the trouble was that every time he felt this way, he would come out feeling more depressed than ever. His life was all but chaotic now and he could hardly tell whether he was going or coming. He was beginning to feel this way when he saw that she was not going but coming.

"Hi," she said, "can I join you?"

"Be my guest," he said, "at your own expense."

Njeri laughed; the winning confident laugh of one who knew her trade.

It was always that way. They never understood that he wanted quiet, that call girls and he had never really hit it off. He remembered fights he'd had several times. He would take his corner to shirk the world and no sooner had he got round to the second bottle than he would look up into padded breasts and sparkling eyes and "Hey," they'd go, "Can I join you?"

They would join him all right, sometimes one, sometimes two or even three. In the dim lights when all girls looked beautiful, he would be flanked between their naked make-believe intimacy.

"Bwana wants some more beer," they called out to the waiter.

But as the night wore on and his pockets wore out (it was only twilight now) they fled to some other victim.

Njeri sat down and her wooden bra tickled him across the table. They couldn't have met before, she said. But there was a certain kind of simplicity about her that seemed to show through the obvious label of her profession.

He knew that it was only one more beer and his reserve was gone. Here was another one Kibonde would envy him tonight.

Njeri knew she had changed a lot. Hers was hard business to be sure but although she was now well in her thirties, she had hardly a care in the world, and that kept her youthful. With her wig and mask of powder only her eyes would perhaps give her away. She spoke 'reasonable' English. Although she could still neither read nor write, she could tell when a ten shilling note wasn't a ten shilling note and that was enough in Gino's. Looking at her now, Mr. Martin was somehow reminded of the haunted look of the boy who was found drowned in his swimming pool earlier that week. The boy had mystified the police as nothing had been taken from the floating handbag.

Mr. Martin did not give it much thought.

Naturally at the back of her mind she still blamed Kibonde for desertion. But she was not emotional about it any more.

"Another?" asked Mr. Martin putting his arm around her.

10

Twilight slowly withdraws and finally disappears. It gets awfully cold and the old man gathers his stool, the snuff box and the few odd things he had taken out of the hut during the day. He locks the small door and lights a big fire for himself as cold steals through the cracks of the mud wall. During the wet season rain gives him no rest. The grass thatched roof is old and far from water-tight so that rain drops sneak in and hang down the stalactite of black soot, strategically.

After hovering there for some time to survey the scene, they locate him; they are now heavy and can no longer hold. Then the old man makes the mistake of looking up at the undependable roof and a timely drop lands in his eye.

The yellow taint gained from the pungent soot feels like pepper and he rubs furiously at his eye. He seems helpless against the rain, everything. But that, at least, is a mercy. For as he curses the roof and swears it will be weighted down with fresh grass just you wait until the dry season his thoughts are — for a moment at any rate — diverted. But it doesn't last. His mind again wanders only to settle at the same old thought.

He is not bitter, only perhaps uneasy, very uneasy. He accepts that Mr. Martin does at least give Njeri more than he, Kibonde, ever gave her. The two had come home together and then she had eventually stayed. It had taken Kibonde some time to recognise her but at least he couldn't mistake those eyes which had now changed, a little coquettishly. Then he had recalled the easy tone of her voice and although she now spoke English, he couldn't misplace that edge to her voice which had once excited him so long ago. Like Mr. Martin he could also see something of the haunted boy's look in her eyes and it made him very uncomfortable.

Perhaps bwana knows about them, perhaps he doesn't But Kibonde had to leave. He could not be servant to her. She had treated him to contemptuous indifference, as if she could hardly be bothered, but only because this was worse than talking. Her eyes told a silent story that was all too indicting, yet unbearably inarticulate. Chance had caught up with them in a vicious and strange style in the house of a white man who had failed in life.

Now at the hill, he cannot help the feeling that the gods must have put in an angry hand when his brothers divided the better land amongst themselves during the Land Consolidation leaving that unwanted hill. He cannot help that feeling when at full moon the ghost of Mbara reflects in the encircling river below and the wind screams at him. He had gone — fled, in fact — back after all these years (as if the City had become suddenly haunted) to the hill he feels like neither living in nor going away from.

With the waters below feeling tighter around his neck, he feels worse as time goes on. He has been reduced to one who looks well beyond his actual years; rugged, pursued by thoughts he cannot impart, hopelessly untidy. Sometimes he feels he would like to go back and hack somebody, anybody to death. But something stronger stays him as if to urge, "you have no right ... no right at all."

sixteen

the clerk

I stopped drawing and stared long at the sleepy messenger. But I wasn't thinking of him. In fact I wasn't thinking of anything in particular. I was just bored. For some reason I was always bored at around eleven in the morning.

The messenger's head drooped and rested comfortably on a large open book of accounts on the table. This wasn't good enough of course. I had to take a firm line. Everything has limits — including the freedom a lazy messenger can enjoy under a tolerant clerk.

"Zakayo!" I snapped.

The head jerked up and two dull eyes stared up at me. The eyes lacked speculation — like those of Banquo's ghost.

I laughed at him, " 'Thou hast no speculation in those eyes Which thou dost glare with!' "

"Nini sema?" As usual Zakayo's voice was hostile. I stopped smiling and curved my lips to a firm line.

"You are a fool to sleep on duty with Mr. Howard just there. Snap out of it."

"Yes?" he sneered, the war spirit lighting up his eyes, "*Mjinga wewe.*"

Hardly the proper way to talk to a clerk, of course, but I was used to this sort of thing.

Weakly I began a speech — rather more to exercise my lame Swahili than to correct a perverse servant.

"Do you know why you are here?" I began. "You are in the service of the bank. You are here in the capacity of a messenger." I paused to let this sink in. "I have often heard you describe yourself as an ambassador which is *Kasia*. You are not a diplomatic representative. You are a servant stationed here so I can send you to and fro according to my wishes. If you act as if — Zakayo! You are asleep again!"

The head jerked up. The eyes duller than ever, quite devoid of speculation, stared into mine.

"*Mjinga wewe!*" he said and with a short laugh fell asleep.

That's the way with banks at the wrong end of the month. Especially small banks. Everybody is crowding at the Statements Counter to see how the "Balance" is doing. No-one seems to want cheque books. At times like these the wise clerk may relax and on bank material write poetry or draw.

"Young man!" a sharp female voice that carried me through history in a moment of time into the stern Victorian Age said, "As soon as you have quite finished scrawling things on that sheet of paper I shall ask for a new cheque book."

Hastily and, I admit, nervously, I threw the sheet into the dustbin. She was a tough customer this. Need I say more? I leave it to you to imagine a tough, fat (or to be polite, plump) lady with a gorgeous hat, a mighty expensive dress and gloves glaring at me through the counter-bars outraged at the indignity of being kept waiting.

"Sorry Ma'am. I — I —" I switched on an apologetic smile. It died on my lips as she remained stony and unmoved.

"I'm always amazed," she said in her loud, carrying voice, "at the shameful decline of service at places of business such as banks. Well, young man? Have you quite finished?"

She handed me her requisition form which I stared at with half seeing eyes. Mabel FitzGerald, I thought... A rich heiress... Or rich widow...

"Well, young man?" her voice was impatient.

"Oh," I said, my mind clicking back to business. "Address... Account Number there... Sig — is this your signature?"

With great tolerance she smiled deliciously.

"What do you think it is?" she asked.

"I thought it was just the — the name," I stammered. I called myself an idiot.

Mabel FitzGerald straightened up with great dignity.

"That has been my usual and normal signature, young man, for the last forty years," she said.

"Quite, quite . . ." I heard myself say. I turned round slowly.

"Zakayo . . . Zakayo!" I said.

The head jerked up.

I handed him the form. "Get it passed. *Fanya haraka,*" I said. The order lacked the usual spark. I had been stripped clean of my dignity.

"Mjinga..." Zakayo said as he rose heavily. His complete disregard of the lady who stood at the other side amazed me. I felt beaten.

While we waited for Zakayo to get the official initial on the form I busied myself by toying with my pen. The lady was reading a notice on the wall... To an artistic eye her profile was tempting . . .

Soon Zakayo returned with the form.

"Fanya haraka!" he said, slapping the thing on the counter. I was used to this too. But in the circumstances — I mean with this particular customer within ear-shot and my mind still confused — I was annoyed. I promised Zakayo a broken neck through a gesture and a calculated look.

I was vigorously stamping her cheque book of sixty leaves (a darn funny size to want at this time of the month) when I heard a sound for which the English don't seem to have a word. You might call it a cry of surprise but it is shorter and more precise. It was a funny strangled sound. I rushed up to see what she had swallowed.

"Ma'am?"

"How did you know?" she demanded, her voice high-pitched.

"Ma'am?"

"How did you do it?" she said.

"Ma'am?"

"Don't stand there saying 'Ma'am, Ma'am!' " she snapped. But her face didn't look hard at all. She looked so surprised. She thrust a sheet of paper under my nose. I took a quick breath. Drawn on it was a pretty young woman of about thirty in a nice hat, an expensive dress and fine gloves. How foolish of me!

"Just tell me," she said, "what were you " — a little lady-like choke — "trying to do?"

I swallowed. "Madam," I said quietly, "I'm sorry. It's force of habit. I've been drawing since I could hold a pencil and I draw something every day of my life." I paused, realising I was in the middle of another speech. "Recently I have taken a keen interest in a new line. Drawing young faces from — er — older ones. I mean, guessing how an old person used to look when young. I mean —"

"It's all right, I get you," she said quietly. She looked at me for a long time and then at the drawing. The softness of her face brought a curious lump into my throat. Suddenly she straightened up.

"Well, what are you waiting for?" she had resumed her stony dignity. "Get on with the cheque book, young man".

Half a minute later, the cheque book ready, she quietly disappeared. And with her the drawing.

"Zakayo," I said that afternoon. "Have you heard of this company calling itself East African Guitars Limited?"

"No."

"You have now."

"Who are they?" Zakayo said with a yawn.

"Lunatics," I said. "They want six one-twenty-leaf cheque books. I'm expected to stamp them all now."

"That's a pity," Zakayo said looking interested.

"It's nothing," I said. "But I have stomach-ache. Stamp them up."

"All right," he said, rising heavily, "how much now . . . Let's see. Six books of one-twenty-"

I slapped a fifty-cents coin on the counter. "That's more than fair," I said firmly, "Take it or leave it."

I settled at a quiet corner hidden from certain eyes and watched with satisfaction as Zakayo settled himself at the stamping hand-machine to fulfil his end of the business. It was a hot afternoon and I felt sleepy. I assumed the attitude of complete concentration upon a cheque leaf.

I will hurry over the next bit because it is not very clear or fresh in my memory. I will start where a bank messenger brought me a small blue envelope in familiar hand-writing. It was addressed to the cheque-book clerk. I couldn't make out whose writing it was but I remember it filled me with a curious thrill of excitement. I tore it open and found a note

"*At exactly five o'clock today,*" I read, "*a dark green Toyota will stop in front of the New Stanley Hotel. A chauffeur in green uniform and a red cap will be driving it. If you get into it, though no explanations have been or will be offered, you may well find yourself in for quite a small fortune.*"

I stared at nothing for a long time. I sat very still. Then I read it again and laughed. This was one of my colleagues playing me tricks.

"Hey, Chege," I said to the bearer of the note, who had lingered on for some conversation with Zakayo. "Who gave you this letter?"

"That letter?" he repeated, "Someone from the President's office."

I stared at him. "Don't be funny!" I said.

"Well, I mean, could be or could not be the President's office. But that car! That smart green uniform. That's it — the President's office."

I didn't blink. I just sat very still — while wave after wave of a wide range of complex feelings flowed through my system. My hands were weak. I felt strangely weak.

That evening a long dark green car stopped in front of a large house, an immense black silhouette against the darkening, glowering sky. The chauffeur got out. So did I — for good or for evil. I had taken a chance (perhaps the chance of a lifetime) and waited for the car according to the instructions in the letter. True to the letter the chauffeur had told me nothing. He had remained a human rock capable only of grunting.

He closed the door of the car and grunted that I follow him. We entered the house.

The room we entered was small but on stepping in a cry of surprise escaped me.

"Who — What — How — I say!" I exclaimed to the rock man. I saw he had gone. But I didn't care.

"They interest you?" said a voice I immediately recognised. Mabel FitzGerald rose from behind a large statue.

"Mrs. FitzGerald," I exclaimed. Then, "Are you an artist?"

She laughed. "Good question. Brings us to the point immediately. And it shows you have art in your blood. I'm surprised you are a clerk."

My heart beat faster. I looked round at the statues and paintings with which the room was crowded. Then at the woman. Could it be that at last — ?

"Can you start work immediately?" she asked.

"Work?"

"Yes, work!" she said. "Come over here."

I was at her side like a shot. Then I stared. She was pointing at a drawing on the canvas. I gaped. The drawing was exactly like the rough one I had done almost unknowingly that morning. Well, it was much larger but that was the only difference.

Mabel FitzGerald looked at me in sudden urgency.

"My only son did that at the age of sixteen. He copied it from an old photograph of mine taken many years ago. This morning you did one exactly like it. I am not superstitious but I believe there's a lot in that. A whole lot. Do you know how to paint pictures?"

"I paint a lot. In water colours — that is." I added hastily looking round at the wonderful oil paintings. "I — why do you ask?"

Mable FitzGerald looked fixedly at me with her hazel eyes. She said:

"I'm an artist. I could start on this picture where my son left off. But the result would be a painting in my style and nothing like my son's work. He died before finishing his work and I have many times wished he had completed this painting of me. I want you to finish this picture. I know you'll paint it exactly the way my son would have done!"

A long time afterwards — how long exactly I don't know — I was fighting. I fought like never before in my life — against an unknown foe. I bit, I screamed, I scratched — and smacked. The foe was trying to take away from me the cheque Mrs. FitzGerald had given me for my work. I clung to it and fought.

"Snap out of it! Snap out of it!" A thunderous voice from the distant hills called with fury as the battle raged.

"Save me!" I cried to the Unseen Intruder, "I'm robbed!"

My foe laughed. It was an uncanny laugh. "He's mad!" he shouted.

"Wake up!" cried the Unseen Intruder very near now. And I was afraid. Afraid of him too.

"Wake up!" he cried.

I opened my eyes with a start.

Zakayo was laughing. The tears streamed down his eyes. Mr. Howard the head of the Deposit Department was glaring down at me. A group of the bank employees stood by looking on in amusement mingled with mystification. And Mary — that's one of the typists — looked horrified.

She helped me up. "Are you all right?" she asked in great concern.

"Of course," I said. "I've just had — a dream. Someone fighting me and so forth."

Zakayo roared afresh. Mr. Howard took a step towards him.

"Shut up!" he cried, "Tell me, what were you doing to this young man before I interfered?"

Zakayo suppressed his laughter enough to be able to speak. "Sir," he said, "He was — ha-ha! He was spoiling the cheque. That one in his hand. He was smiling in a dream and rolling it in his hand. When I came up to take it from him — wow! ha! wow! He was the tiger, the untame lion. Ha! ha! wow — !"

It was a good joke. And he didn't laugh alone. The rest though not really understanding it all joined in. Except Mary of course, who — But that is neither here nor there.

If anyone knows a Mabel FitzGerald contact me and give me her address so I can tell her thanks awfully. Not that I never heard from her again after that morning. A few days later I received by registered mail a generous number of bank notes. With the money was this note.

"Dear Clerk,

In my hurry last Monday I took with me one of your works of art — the picture of the young lady in a hat. Perhaps the enclosed will settle that little matter.

Mabel FitzGerald."

And I would like to tell Mabel FitzGerald thanks awfully.

seventeen

the potent ash

"Karo! Karo! Karo!"

For the first time the youth knew fear. Dread of something strange and powerful. Unfelt and uncanny, like a myriad snakes in the dark approaching, but unapproachable. It was not just the fearfulness that stole into the imagination of boyhood flung into hostile loneliness by the tribe. Such he had known two nights ago. He had then been afraid of what he could feel tangibly, something vulnerable like himself which he could see, grip and fight. But this *was* fear; and he was not even running. There was nowhere to run. He could only submit.

Karo staggered out of the darkness of his lone grass hut into the darkness of the world outside. Hardly moving, he looked up. He could see nothing. His eyelids closed and pressed. The cloud of tears rolled out along the corners and he could now see the stars cast high and still in the vast night. They seemed to answer his silent plea with taunting winks, mocking and condemning him as everyone and everything were doing. He held fast . . . moaning.

"Karo!" the spirits called again. The muffled voices echoed and beat savagely against the walls of the deep, barren valley of the dead and the owls.

Frightened, Karo dropped his head. He clasped his hands at his chest and regarded the chilling darkness of the valley beneath.

"I am coming!" he cried. He knew they were too far to hear him. Only the valley of the ancestors mocked back echoes of his own voice, "Coming, coming..." He felt naked against the rushing wind for a goatskin slip was all he wore. He gathered it tighter around his waist. Then he began his journey.

His steps were blind, quick and careless. He felt himself dragged by its steepness, hurried on as if everything was whirling, rolling him on for a fateful meeting.

They called incessantly, and although he knew they still could not hear his weak voice he answered as he stumbled on. The matted grass tore at his feet, the dead thorn trees cut and thrashed at his body until he stopped. He had hit himself against a massive tree.

Again he looked up. He bled from the cuts and blood mingled with sweat. No longer did the stars mock him. They now hid in fear behind an angry cloud which crept and hovered over him like the wing of a giant eagle. Amidst the calls of his ancestors, he heard a distant owl cry.

"Karo!" It was now a shrilling single voice that called. It did not wait for him to answer. "Why did you not come the first night we called?"

The voice, say the cry, was bitter and bit deep into the valley. A female voice? It drowned every other noise as if consuming the whole valley into itself. Would he throw himself prostrate before a female ghost? But had ghosts shape or sex?

"Answer!"

"I — I was afraid," he said.

"Afraid? Do you not want to meet your fathers now that they are dead and bodiless?"

He did not answer. He flung his arms round the tree, burying his head down against it . . . . and moaned.

"Did I call yesternight? Didn't your ancestor's voice defy the thunder and the rain, the whisper of the winds, *just* to reach you? Did it? Did I?"

"You did...... you did...... please do not......"

He would stop there, arms flung around the tree, and let them come for him. But perhaps they might understand. Something urged him on, said he must exonerate himself to the spirits. They must not lay their hand upon him so heavily, so cruelly. He had not hit in cold blood. He had only been defending himself as he had been forced to do ever since he could remember.

Again they called, and again he plunged his feet into the blind darkness. He tripped over and fell for the fourth time. He became more scared. It spelt bad luck to fall more than three times while on a journey. A lucky journey indeed! He stumbled and fell yet again, almost deliberately. Could the superstition of the tribe serve him worse than the Sacred Arena?

"How old are you?" asked a voice.

"He came to the tribe during the Famine of the Many," chuckled another. "Barely a man, but old enough to know better."

"Old enough for blood to answer blood? . . . . Listen Karo."

Listen. The very tone echoed in his confused mind his uncle's warning one evening long ago in the hut.

"Listen and remember my boy", the old man had said as he blew furiously at the glowing logs to set them into flames. "Watch out for malice. Malice against you, your adopted half-sisters and brothers of the clan......"

"But I do not understand," Karo had said looking into the old man's eyes. He saw them reflect angrily and red the flames which now roared and flickered in little explosive sounds as they devoured the helpless logs.

"I know you cannot. You are hardly old enough, but you must put on a man's armour."

It was then at that early age that Karo realised he was different. He learnt why the other boys avoided him in fight or play. Why his world of contact was confined to his uncle and his mother. She would not want him to know that she was not his real mother, that he was illegitimate, that he belonged to another tribe. His mother had been barely more than a girl at his birth and his real far-away tribe beyond the hills would not tolerate such side-stepping of rigid morals. She had stamped shame on the clan. Their custom demanded that the girl's clan cast away the child on the No-man's-land along the river dividing them and Urabi's tribe. There it could survive or die. It did not matter which. At least they had pacified the wrathful gods.

Luck (the adopted clan cried "shame and misfortune") played a hand. Grazing his cattle by the river, Urabi spotted two women running away. He drew closer, and at last heard the cry of the child. Something appealed to him in the innocence of the cry. He recalled bitterly the fate his favourite sister Nara had suffered because the clan believed it was unlucky to have twins. He thought of her. Nara who was beautiful and kind — at least once beautiful, but kind even now. But she had suffered childlessness and became the laughing stock of other women. And once she did have children, they had been twins. Perhaps, Urabi thought, she might care for the child. Since her misfortune he had come to reject the curse of superstition being extended to innocence such as he beheld in the child. Was the infant to account to the gods for its mother's morality or immorality?

Nara loved the child passionately. So forcefully in fact that she fell out with all her people except Urabi. (With her husband of course she had fallen out long before. She was not, he bragged, the only woman in his polygamous quiver.) It was bad enough to adopt another woman's child unless the mother was a dead relative. But it begged damnation to care for the life of an enemy tribe. Later, however, her own tribe had come to tolerate her if only because they reservedly respected her brother Urabi.

She had approached the medicine man. But they knew better than that. No witchdoctor would risk severing the chain of fate which blessed his trade by attempting to cleanse the child. He was alien and not of their tribe's temper. Even if they tried, the child would still be impossible. They could not burn out with the smoke of the ram on the furnace under the fig-tree, the dark, destructive fire glowing within him. After the devil within had burnt to ashes there would remain not cold and powerless ash, but ash which revived its malice. He was the ash that lay so cold and dead in their hearths, and yet when they used it in their food for flavour, it came alive in their mouths with a taste salty, almost pungent. Potent ash that in sickly wind blew unseen, unannounced like a shadow, creeping everywhere into everything. His adopted clan and tribe would suspect and curse him with every cow that died; with every period of drought; with the ill wind which in dry weather carried destructive, ravaging fire from hut to hut. And with every woman who became childless, they would remember and curse, and spit scorn.

Now Urabi who understood him was dead, long dead. Was it possible, yes, was it not possible that it was his voice that now muffled with the others of his ancestors in the dark valley saying again,

"Listen..... Do you know the voice speaking to you?"

"No."

"No? Why is the ash condemned to the Sacred Arena where even the wind would not dare blow it from?"

He did not say a word.... He moaned.

"Answer!"

"I killed a man."

"Why may one not come near the ash except in the valley of the forefathers?"

"Because I killed.... killed.... killed!" he cried.

"Why did you kill *me?*"

It was like a loud whisper, a husky voice which thrust and cut a cold shudder down his back. This could not be Naima's voice. But was Naima not a spirit now?

"Do you hit a man when he is down?"

He had not meant to kill him. They had had a minor quarrel, in itself a triviality. But he had continued to hit and pound even after the other lay unconscious. It was not bitterness against Naima. It was as if in treading him into the mud, he had triumphed for a fateful moment over a cruel people who had been imposed upon him but who always cursed the devils for imposing him upon them. He had released through each blow the foam of inhibited bitterness bubbling within. At last inarticulation had worn bitter expression. His uncle had told him to use his armour. But he had also used against Naima, his arrow, hitting deep into his opponent. And yet, this triumph was, ironically, the lonely hole from which he could never hope to rise to the surface again. The act had rendered him powerless, for the bee had stung once in its victim and could not sting again.

He knew what lay in their hungry hands. It was the excuse they needed. But he would not let them. He must escape to the Sacred Arena by the valley where only the ostracised would dare to step. That was two nights ago, and this night he knew he must submit.

"Do you hit a downed man?" the question was repeated.

"You attacked me first," Karo gathered strength to answer, "if I had let you up again, you would have killed me."

"Shut up, blundering calabash."

Karo stumbled on, down and down, all the time feeling he should go back. But there it still was, urging him on, saying he must be given a chance to explain.

Now the valley became completely silent, and Karo found himself borne deeper and lonelier in its vastness. Even the wind struck condemning notes on his ears.

"Do you know what an evil spell you have cast on the clan by your act?" a voice asked now disturbing the pregnant quiet which hung in the valley with potent meaning.

"I know I have done them wrong," he said weakly.

"Wrong! Be damned." The clamorous echo of the roar cut across the valley with unmistakable fury. "Nara is dead."

"Dead!" Karo let out the word in choked breath. Yet again he flanked himself against a large boulder for support.

He knew they would eventually drive her to it. Ever since he could remember they were doing it. Once they had him, they had Nara too, for there would now be nothing left for her to live for.

"Their goats and cattle have been stolen and the whole

clan impoverished. Your aunt has had twins which the clan cast away after your spell this morning."

He did not want to approach further. He was only twenty paces from the region of the voice.

"Why do you stop?"

"Why do you kill me this way, call me every night?" he asked. "I want to explain . . ."

"You will come here!" all the voices cut through the darkness in a deep simultaneous rumble.

This time he obeyed and slouched weakly closer. There was no movement except that of his feet.

The wind stood still.

Suddenly, a hand fell in his. It was a warm hand, its grip almost friendly. The hand led him into a tunnel which twisted ominously in a steep descent. At last they reached the basement and his feet slipped on the loose earth. He could not tell how many there were, these ghosts. A torch glowed several paces to the left, shedding its light like the dawn sun. It gave him hope of being understood.

"I want to explain", he pleaded as if in answer. But no one spoke to him. The walls of the ill-lit cave shot out deadly echoes of his voice from distant walls. Then silence, cold and hostile, reigned once more.

Moment upon moment passed. Still, silence reigned. Then somebody said "Here no one will know". Could these after all be Naima's relatives who had sworn to avenge him? Had they not asked, "why may one not come near the ash except in the valley of the forefathers?" The torch now seemed to be burning away and weaker in the distance. It was like the sun at dusk, yielding its twilight warmth into the mounting cold of night. With it, that hope of being given a flicker of a chance to explain burnt away.

"Your blood and ours be forever apart!" they shouted all at once.

And as he fell, Karo knew that his adopted clan had decided to bury the ash away forever.

eighteen

letter to the haunting past

You came to me last night, in the phantom face of my great grandfather; as you did the night before, and the night before that. In my nakedness, I could see your point as you drew back your bow to splash another quiver into my subconscious. You refused to sit on my bed as you talked, refused to step on my floor, and just hovered there in the air, saying everything from me to my flat spelt betrayal, the air smelt burial, something was gone. And I, mesmerised, lay on dumb.

I never knew you, never met you. Awake, I now find the ancestral herald so distant. But I feel that behind the facade of fury which you so freely displayed last night, deep within, you were never one to let emotion take the bull by the horns. I do not know much about the old wine. From the cradle the better part has drunk of the new gourd. But I do know, do feel it in me, that between us, between my nostalgia for you and the reality of the moment, between the incantation of the witchdoctor's magic wand and the bible, between your arrow and my pen, swirls, yet in the contrast, the thick lifeblood; so that you and I revolve in a tied history.

As you dealt your condemning plea, I could tell your questions unequivocally bid the impossible. For how can I, so involved in what you term aimless struggle, go back? Here I am, groping paddle in hand, pledged to blend in the mortar the ethnic of the native and the exotic grain. In the dark chaos of my endeavour, is it a wonder that I am, as you bitterly accused, the penumbra, the black sheep of a finer and gone society? But no, wait: Gone .... yes; but Finer? Well, is this not the irrationalism of nostalgia? I have lately had this sentiment hurled full face at me in the abstract of socialism and nationalism, and in the current mass aversion to things foreign.

Am I to answer for the penumbra, the groping half-way, transitory self? You were there on the advent and disembowelling scramble of the foreign victor. You saw for yourself how the harmattan swept through the land with the fire of gospel, cannon and guile, to dispel the former ways, putting to flight with penicillin the devil out of the witch-doctor's tool. You *were* there when the old met the new . . . and gave way.

I know how you feel about the bitter earth. For a pinch of salt, the touch of calico instead of the old leopard outfit, my ancestry put on the green light to towns, bits and things, the lot.

You let me know last night that not all of this new wine tasted stale, and I was gratified. Hovering over me in ethereal fury, however, you would not forgive me for this spiritually-lost self. I yield to the arrow. I also am appalled to witness, cast off the reins, gods who would never declare perfection but who, at least, in the spell of the fig-tree and the mountain won belief from a deep, honest heart. In the saddle now reigns a powerful ten commandment giant of faith to which the native rebel in me clings only through fear. A faith which, outside the theory of the sabbath house, front-rows the white with God, huddles the black into the pit with the demons, and continues to play in its vast christian amphi-theatre, the pain and misery of inherent racialism. And this to spark off the envy of the gods (Alas, Gods) of Kirinyagas within the hearts of black souls! Here they came, clad in priestly robes, the same testament in hand, and on two hills erected two camps which would see eye to eye neither with you, nor with each other. The one Catholic and the other protesting a cleaner stand, their pulpit lured in the crafty manner of the politician's dance. Now the native in me is torn child of two worlds in spiritual confusion and want. And Allah's spirit will only aggravate.

You spat the vehement spit of scorn and bid that I look at the youth of the day. I know we have failed you. The reality of the urban day alive with anxiety, idleness and ignorance; the grandeur of the nocturnal neon and the brothel harlot for the escapist — these have yielded in my fellow urban youth a certain barrenness, a lamentable moral depravity for which you now indict me. I do not mean to exonerate them. But as they experiment and play the forlorn beat generation to the tune of the imported leather jacket, the tightness of the wee knee-high skirt, and the skin lightening cream of the ashamed (ashamed at you, their Past), I know that somewhere deep inside lurks the reservoir of good craving for an outlet, a direction, but only untapped in the brainwashing escapism of ephemeral novelties.

You will lure me again tonight, incarnate spirits, but I shall not now remain silent. For this is my decision: that I will not come with you. I really do not decline the ride back along the exciting path of negritude, a path swept moist with the sweat of Senghor's black muse. It is that I cannot discard into the commitment of your black rubicon, the fairer of the grains lying in the mortar, for both have become a part of me. Here shall I stay and strive to yield shape to this transitory embryo.

I can see your scorn as you point your arrow at the negative in the politician's round-table and ask, "Is this how?" Well, here is the soft spot which hurts. Hurts at the emptiness of paper talk which conceals the lie in cocktail occasions and yields nothing real to reinspire the native ego.

But, dear Past, we shall triumph yet. In the Ibo tribes of a myriad Things Fall Apart, in Afric wide fountains of Nigeria Mbari, in voices vindicated we shall soon be Facing Mount Kenya with confidence. Therein shall the heart surmount The River Between and throb tempo once more to the drums of the poetic hills retuned to weave pregnant rhythm to the lyrics of re-discovered dignity from the Atlas to the Tables.

My prayer, one, is that wound to a new line, I shall divorce this complex which pains the mind, as the new world in a pose condescending and, at best, patronizing, reflects my other face in that herald ancestral....

But I await his errand again now, as I withdraw, with the dark night, into the stillness of my room.

Published by the East African Publishing House, Koinange Street, P.O. Box 30571, Nairobi and printed in letterpress by afropress ltd., P.O. Box 30502, Saldanha Lane, Nairobi, Kenya.

